PRAISE FO

Here are some of the over 100,000 five star reviews left for the Dead Cold Mystery series.

"Rex Stout and Michael Connelly have spawned a protege."

AMAZON REVIEW

"So begins one damned fine read."

AMAZON REVIEW

"Mystery that's more brain than brawn."

AMAZON REVIEW

"I read so many of this genre...and ever so often I strike gold!"

AMAZON REVIEW

"This book is filled with action, intrigue, espionage, and everything else lovers of a good thriller want."

AMAZON REVIEW

FIRE FROM HEAVEN
A DEAD COLD MYSTERY

BLAKE BANNER

RIGHTHOUSE

Copyright © 2024 by Right House

All rights reserved.

The characters and events portrayed in this ebook are fictitious. Any similarity to real persons, living or dead, is coincidental and not intended by the author.

No part of this book may be reproduced in any form or by any electronic or mechanical means, including information storage and retrieval systems, without written permission from the author, except for the use of brief quotations in a book review.

ISBN-13: 978-1-63696-010-4

ISBN-10: 1-63696-010-3

Cover design by: Damonza

Printed in the United States of America

www.righthouse.com

www.instagram.com/righthousebooks

www.facebook.com/righthousebooks

twitter.com/righthousebooks

DEAD COLD MYSTERY SERIES
An Ace and a Pair (Book 1)
Two Bare Arms (Book 2)
Garden of the Damned (Book 3)
Let Us Prey (Book 4)
The Sins of the Father (Book 5)
Strange and Sinister Path (Book 6)
The Heart to Kill (Book 7)
Unnatural Murder (Book 8)
Fire from Heaven (Book 9)
To Kill Upon A Kiss (Book 10)
Murder Most Scottish (Book 11)
The Butcher of Whitechapel (Book 12)
Little Dead Riding Hood (Book 13)
Trick or Treat (Book 14)
Blood Into Wine (Book 15)
Jack In The Box (Book 16)
The Fall Moon (Book 17)
Blood In Babylon (Book 18)
Death In Dexter (Book 19)
Mustang Sally (Book 20)
A Christmas Killing (Book 21)
Mommy's Little Killer (Book 22)
Bleed Out (Book 23)

Dead and Buried (Book 24)
In Hot Blood (Book 25)
Fallen Angels (Book 26)
Knife Edge (Book 27)
Along Came A Spider (Book 28)
Cold Blood (Book 29)
Curtain Call (Book 30)

ONE

It was sunny and warm, so we had the windows down in the Jag. We were following East Tremont all the way down to the East River. East Tremont is a very long avenue, so we were relaxing and cruising. Occasionally I would glance at Dehan. She was smiling behind her mirrored aviators, with strands of hair whipping across her face.

"Talk me through it," I said.

"Well, as I see it"—she showed me a lot of teeth—"you're Agent Mulder and I am Agent Scully..."

"Be serious. We're almost there."

"Be serious?" She raised an eyebrow. "Okay. Danny Brown, aged twenty, found dead at the south end of Soundview Park, near the mouth of the Bronx River, on Monday, the eighth of June, 1998. Cause of death..." She fingered some strands of hair from her mouth and tied her hair into a knot at the back of her head. "The ME was unable to establish a cause of death because the body..." She raised her shades onto the top of her head like a medieval visor so that she could squint at me. "... had been incinerated from his ankles to his neck. I don't get that."

"Just keep going. We'll have a chance to review the details."

She sighed. "Okay. His feet were not burned. They were standing, facing the river, in a pair of flip-flops."

I raised an eyebrow. "Thongs."

She shook her head. "No, Stone. A thong is something else. We have been over this. We are going to call them flip-flops."

I grunted. "There was some burning around the ankles, but the *thongs* were unmelted, despite the heat needed to incinerate the body."

"Who's talking who through this?"

"Whom. You are. Me. You are talking me through it. Continue."

"The ME said that the legs had been severed at the ankle with surgical precision. There was no damage to the cartilage or the joints, other than the singeing. The same was true of the head. This was lying on the grass about eighteen inches from the body, as though it had rolled. There was singeing on the cut, which was also surgical in precision, and there was no damage to the vertebrae—again, other than singeing. Finally, the genitals had also been surgically removed—or at least removed with surgical precision . . ."

"Correct. Good. We do not know that they were surgically removed, only that they were removed, in a way we do not know, with surgical precision."

"That was my point, Stone. That's why I said it."

I grinned at her. "Good."

"They too were singed and placed roughly in the correct position. The rest of his body was ash, with a few pieces of bone."

I nodded. "Those bones corresponded to . . ."

She interrupted. "I was coming to that." She closed her eyes. "Pieces of rib, collarbone, upper arm, thigh, and tibia, suggesting the body had not burned at an even temperature. However, all the bits of bone were found in the correct location on the body. That would be consistent with the body's having burned *in situ*."

I turned right into Schurz Avenue, opposite the Marina Del Rey, and asked, "Problems with that possibility?"

"Well, for a start, the heat needed to incinerate a body to little more than ash, in an open location, like a park, would be insane. Generating that kind of heat in a park would be almost impossible, plus, that kind of heat should have burned his feet, his head, and his balls, and all the grass around him."

"Unless...?"

She sighed. "Unless it was a laser. Which we both know it wasn't."

"I don't know that and neither do you."

She ignored me. "Also, it rained on Sunday night, but there were no footprints approaching or leaving the location where the body was found. Stone, you cannot seriously be considering..."

"I am not seriously considering anything at the moment, Little Grasshopper. My mind is open. All I know, like Mr. Socrates, is that I know nothing."

I turned right again into Brinsmade Avenue and pulled up outside Detective Arnaldo Ochoa's house. It was a redbrick box with a front lawn enclosed by a tubular metal fence with chicken wire stretched across it. All in all the effect was ugly, but he obviously took pride in his garden, because that was well tended, with a handsome chestnut on one side and a small vegetable patch on the other.

He came out to greet us before we'd reached the door. He was a friendly, smiling guy who looked unnaturally boyish for his sixty-two years of age. There was a kind of eagerness to his eyes when he smiled, as though he really wanted you to smile back. He held out his hand. "Stone, son of a gun, how're you doing? You still the man at the precinct? I thought you'd be captain by now!"

I shook his hand. "Arn, this is my partner, Carmen Dehan. She's the one who stopped me making captain. Everybody hates her."

He laughed. She didn't. "Come on out back, we'll have more privacy there. What can I get you? Lemonade? Beer?"

He led us out to a backyard that was as well tended as the front. He had a small patio with a garden table and chairs sitting in the dappled shade of a plane tree. On the table there was a glass jug of lemonade. He gestured us to a couple of chairs and poured before he too sat. The sun was turning from warm to hot. Somewhere there was a bee getting busy on some flowers, and there was a powerful smell of freshly cut grass.

He shook his head, still smiling. "So you got cold cases, huh?" He turned to Dehan. "Guy was on fire, you know? Real smart, but a bad attitude. Most people didn't like him. But we were okay, right, Stone? I got you. I knew what you were about. You're a good man." He turned back to Dehan. "He's a good man. Am I wrong?"

She gave a slow shrug. "If you like opinionated dinosaurs, he's okay. He gets the job done. What can I tell you?"

He laughed out loud. "She's got your number, Stone. Opinionated dinosaur. That's good." He laughed again and shook his head. "So you're looking at the Danny Brown case. Man, I don't know what to tell you about that. I lost sleep over that case. I never saw anything like it. I brought it home with me. I still have it, and you know what? Sometimes I pull it out and I sit there in the evening, looking at it, going over it. It defies explanation."

I sipped my lemonade. "Tell me about Danny. What kind of kid was he?"

"He was a good kid. Everybody seemed to like him. He'd taken a year out to think about what he wanted to do, and his parents were cool with that. They were a pretty cool couple, progressive, liberal . . . At the time of his death, he was studying law. His grades were okay, he was happy, his parents were happy. But here's the thing." He looked from me to Dehan and back again, then repeated, "Here's the thing. The kid was obsessed with UFOs and with that TV series *The X-Files*. You know the kind of thing—posters on his walls, all the DVDs, he'd watched every episode God knows how many times. Every book and magazine article ever published on the Roswell incident, Area 51, he'd read them all. What I'm saying, a total nerd. His obsession with the subject was what made him take the year out, and it was bringing his grades down from very good to just okay. That was his parents' opinion."

Dehan asked, "Is that what he was doing out in the park at night?"

He nodded. "I think so, Carmen. Especially in light of what happened later."

"What do you mean?"

"Well, the lights..."

Dehan frowned at me. She had only read the case file and the case file made no mention of the lights, and I had not mentioned them to her. I said, "Yeah, tell us about the lights."

"I didn't see them, but there were a hell of a lot of witnesses who did. This was on the Sunday night..."

I interrupted, "Before the rain had started, or after?"

He looked surprised. "I'm not sure, John. I'd have to check. If it had started, I don't think it could have been heavy, because a lot of people gathered to watch, along O'Brien Avenue and other places, because you could see them for miles! And I don't think they would have done that if the rain was heavy."

Dehan was frowning. "What kind of lights?"

"Well, from the descriptions I have heard, there were flashing lights, red, yellow, blue, some people say green..."

She snapped, "Red, blue, and yellow, that's a chopper! And the green is an illusion where the blue and the yellow mix."

He gave a small, apologetic laugh. "Yeah, maybe, and lasers that were projected down into the park, at approximately the spot where Danny's body was found."

She raised an eyebrow, picked up her glass and sipped, and somehow made it all suggest he was out of his mind. He spread his hands. "You can read the reports in the local papers, Carmen. And when you talk to the witnesses they will all tell you. I don't dispute that there may well be a perfectly reasonable explanation, but I wasn't able to find it. And the lights were there. That is a fact."

I said, "So these lights were above the park."

FIRE FROM HEAVEN | 5

"At first, yeah. Then, according to the testimony of the witnesses, the lights moved out over the East River, there was a flash of light, and they vanished."

"What color?"

He frowned at me. "You sure ask some funny questions, John. Um, I'm not sure. I'll check, but I think it was just white light."

Dehan looked at me like she wanted to slap some sense into me and said, "So what about the body?"

"So, it's seven thirty on Monday morning when we get the call. This woman is out walking the dog in the morning and she finds the body. Fortunately, she managed to get to the dog before it disturbed anything. This is '98, before everybody had cell phones, so she has to hurry home to call it in. We get there with the crime scene guys and the ME and, believe me, there was not a person there who had ever seen anything like it. It was the craziest fuckin' thing I ever saw in my whole career—in my entire *life*! No exaggeration." He looked at each of us in turn. "For a start." He adjusted his ass in his chair and held out his hands like he was framing a shot in a movie. "There's his feet. They're there, on the grass, about shoulder width apart. Just like he's been standing there looking out at the river. And he's still wearing his fucking thongs."

Dehan smiled. "What are they, like, rubber sandals?"

"Yeah, you know, with the bit that goes between your toes. Like they wear in Florida. His fuckin' head is there, and his fuckin' *balls* are there. Everything, you know, in the right place if you know what I mean. And everything else, his neck, his chest, his arms, his hands, his fuckin' legs—*everything*—has been incinerated. It's just fuckin' ash, you know what I'm saying? Ash! Except there were a few bits of bone, but they were all in the right place where they were supposed to be. It was like, and I don't care if you think I'm crazy because now I'm retired so I can be crazy if I want to, it was exactly like he had been standing there and he had been hit—*zap!*—with a laser."

Dehan sighed and shook her head. I scratched my chin. He

raised both hands and nodded a lot. "I know. I know what you are thinking. It was set up to look that way by some nut. Now, I am going to tell you two things. One . . ." He held up one finger and stared at Dehan. "What possible motive could anybody have to set up such an elaborate, difficult murder? I mean, leave aside for now *how* they did it. We can come back to that in a minute. What possible motive? I mean, that kind of scenario, where the killer sets up an elaborate scene like that after the murder, we only find that with serial killers, right? That is the typical scene where you find that kind of staging of the corpse. But can you think of a single other case where we found a body set up like that?"

Dehan grimaced and I shook my head.

He went on, "Well believe me, I have canvassed every single PD from San Diego to Madawaska, and the only cases like it are unsolved cases of either spontaneous combustion or cattle mutilation." He gave Dehan a challenging smile. "So I ain't the only cop who couldn't solve it. These cases do happen, they are investigated by local PDs, sheriff's departments, *and* the FBI, and they don't get solved."

Dehan looked unhappy. I closed my eyes to think. Ochoa went on. "And two, despite the rain that night, *there were no footprints*! So what are we saying? The body was carefully laid out using a sky crane that nobody noticed?" He leaned forward toward Dehan. "The problem you begin to face, Carmen, is that in order to give this a . . ." He used his fingers to make speech marks. "'Logical' explanation, you have to go to such lengths, to such extremes, that the logical explanation becomes more crazy than the illogical one." He flopped back in his chair, smiling and shaking his head. "His body was surgically incinerated. Get that, *surgically incinerated*! Only a laser can do that, and several hundred people saw a laser at *that* location around the time he must have died."

He spread his hands. Dehan looked at me resentfully. "We have maybe a thousand cold cases, and you have to pick this one."

I gave her my blandest smile. "Just because you are murdered by a bad guy from Betelgeuse doesn't mean you're not entitled to justice, Dehan." I turned to him. "What was your impression of the witnesses . . ."

He snorted. "Such as they were. You say witnesses, but the fact is there weren't any. There were several hundred people who saw the lights that night. But nobody saw the killing. His friends and family, the last people to see him alive. They all liked him, they were all real upset, they all struck me as honest people . . ." He gave a knowing laugh. "In as much as anybody is truly honest, right? But most important of all, there was nobody who had anything you could call a motive." He shook his head. "Nobody had means or motive. It was a locked room mystery, out in the middle of the park."

We were silent for a moment. Finally I asked him, "What is your own feeling? Never mind facts or evidence or lack thereof. What does your gut tell you?"

He smiled at me but pointed at Dehan. "She's going to laugh at me. But Donald Kirkpatrick, who knew Danny really well—he was one of the last people to see him alive—he wrote a book about the case. He called it *Heaven's Fire*. And he says that Danny was shot by a UFO, just like we have assholes who go over to Africa and hunt from helicopters. He figures that's what happened to Danny. He was hunted, for game." He made a face and shrugged. It was an almost apologetic gesture. "I have to say, I agree. After twenty years turning this case over and following every conceivable lead, in my expert opinion, Danny Brown was shot, for sport, by an alien."

TWO

STUART AND MAY BROWN, DANNY'S PARENTS, LIVED across the Westchester Creek in Clason Point. They were both retired—he had been an architect and she a schoolteacher—and, though they sounded surprised on the phone, they were happy for us to drop in. We came off the Bruckner Boulevard onto White Plains Road and then took a right onto Lacombe Avenue. Theirs was a big, yellow detached clapboard affair near the corner with Beach Avenue. We pushed through the wrought iron gate and climbed the five steps to their front door. I pressed the bell and heard it buzz inside. The sun was approaching its zenith and it was getting warm. Dehan stared at me while we waited. I said, "It's almost beer time."

She nodded and the door opened.

Stuart Brown was tall and lean. He had short sandy hair turning to gray and balding on top, like a Franciscan monk. He wore a khaki shirt, with an incongruous Christmas tank top over it, and boot cut jeans. He smiled at us, but it was nothing personal. He looked as though smiling was a habit for him, his go-to response.

"Detectives Stone and Dehan?" We showed him our badges and he gestured us in. "Please, come in, but I am sure I don't know how we can help you. *May!*" This last was hollered up the stairs as we crossed the entrance hall toward his living room. "*May! It's the cops!*" He smiled a smile that would have been cheeky in a child but in him looked like retarded adolescence. "Forgive me," he said. "Go right on in and make yourselves comfortable. May will be down in a moment. Can I offer you anything?"

I took a deep breath, in sympathy with his lungs, and said, "Thank you, no, we really won't keep you long."

We entered an open-plan living room and dining room, with a bow window on the right overlooking the street and a set of French doors at the back, in the dining area, overlooking a backyard. There was a suite of well-used furniture set around a large coffee table, and against one wall in the dining area there was a huge stripped pine dresser. Stuart directed me to sit in a worn, red calico armchair, and Dehan sat on a sofa that was covered in Mexican rugs and bits of newspaper. Feet hurried noisily down the stairs and May Brown came in on short, plump legs that were accustomed to terrorizing noisy classrooms. The rest of her was as short and formidable as her legs, she too had a habitual smile that meant nothing, and, for a moment, I was transfixed by the bizarre image of these two, retired, in each other's company all day, perpetually grinning at each other without meaning it.

"Detective!" she said, reaching for Dehan with both hands. "Don't get up! I'll sit next to you. What is this about? I am fascinated."

Stuart smiled at me. "Welcome to the Age of Aquarius." He turned to his wife, who had sat beside Dehan, grabbed hold of her hand, and was telling her New York needed more strong women, and said, "Darling, this is Detective Stone, Detective Dehan's partner."

She looked at me like I was the unwanted guest at Thanksgiving. "Of course," she said, with big lips and big eyes. I thought she was going to add, "How nice of you to come," but instead she turned back to Dehan and said, "Stuart and I are intrigued, not to say bemused. It has been twenty years! I believe you run a *cold-case* unit...?"

Stuart sat in the armchair opposite me and crossed one long, thin leg over the other. "That suggests that the case is still open," he said. "But, to be honest, to us it is quite definitely closed."

I frowned. "Closed? How could it be? His murderer was never found."

He shook his head, and May stared at me with eyes the color of over-chlorinated swimming pools. "That is absurd. Forgive me for being blunt, Detective, but only the narrow mind of an officious, white male policeman could possibly fail to see what happened to Danny."

I raised an eyebrow at her. "Are you telling me you know what happened, Mrs. Brown? We will consider any explanation that is properly supported by facts."

She waved a small, plump hand at me. "There you go, you see, 'properly supported by facts.'" She sighed. "As far as we are concerned, Detectives, Danny was shot with some sort of energy beam by trans-dimensional beings, or beings from another planet."

I nodded. "I am aware of that theory, Mrs. Brown, but have you anything concrete in the way of facts that I can take to my inspector, so that we can begin extradition proceedings?"

It went straight over May's head. Dehan clenched her jaw and Stuart cocked an eyebrow at me. "We didn't invite you here to mock us, Detective. We are not alone in believing in the presence of trans-dimensional and extraterrestrial beings among us. There are some very eminent minds who accept the possibility."

I nodded. "I'm not mocking you, Mr. Brown, far from it. But I would like you to understand that the NYPD can't just walk away from a homicide investigation because the murder may have been committed by an extraterrestrial."

"Have you read Donald Kirkpatrick's book on the case?"

"No."

"I suggest you do. His investigation is somewhat more thorough than the NYPD's, I am bound to say. His analysis of the situation is profound and comprehensive, and he shows, quite conclusively, Detective Stone, that our son's murder could not have been carried out—mark my words here—*could not have been carried out* by a human being. Once you establish that point, where do you go from there . . . ?"

Dehan scratched her head and spoke. "That's the second time Donald Kirkpatrick's name has come up. What exactly was his relationship to Danny?"

He sank back in his deep chair and brushed some imaginary dust from his blue jeans. "'Relationship' is an unnecessarily strong word, Detective Dehan. They had no *relationship* other than that Donald ran the investigation group in which Danny was involved, along with at least a dozen other people."

I said, "UFOs were a consuming interest for him . . ."

"It was a passion. For May and myself it had been a lifelong interest, but for Danny it was a true passion. We encouraged him but always urged him to approach the subject empirically. Sadly, for the vast majority of ufologists these days, the subject has become religion by another name. And John Mack, for all his good intentions, was, I am afraid, largely to blame."

He said this apologetically, as though I might be scandalized by the suggestion. I shook my head. "John Mack?"

"Professor of psychology at Harvard University, wrote several books on abduction syndrome, concluded that . . ."

"Forgive me, Mr. Brown, we are on the clock and I am sure you have lots to do yourself. What about the other members of the UFO group? How did Danny get on with them? Do any relationships stand out as either particularly good or particularly bad?"

May sighed and shook her head. "Truly, Detective Stone, it is a shame you can't understand you are barking up the wrong tree . . ."

"Help me to understand."

"Danny was gregarious, outgoing, emotionally *very* healthy.

He had all the self-assurance of the only child, which was a deliberate decision on . . ." She nodded graciously at her husband. ". . . our part. The result was that everybody loved him. He was popular, fun, charismatic. He had a *great* sense of humor, didn't he, Stuart?"

Before Stuart could answer, I cut in. "I am sure he was a charming person, Ms. Brown. But, as I am sure you know, the motive for murder lies always in a relationship—whatever the basis of that relationship may be—so at the moment we are keen to understanding all of Danny's relationships. Did he, for example, have a girlfriend?"

She placed both her hands on her lap and affected a loud, parrotlike laugh. "Just one?" She hooted again. "You have photographs of him? He was *gorgeous*! And that happy-go-lucky personality! The girls were crazy about him!" She shook her head. "But he was not ready to settle . . . Hold on."

She rose and strutted on those powerful legs to the dresser in the dining room. There she squatted down with startling flexibility and opened one of the cupboards in the base. She extracted a couple of photo albums and brought them back with her, leafing through the top one as she walked.

She sat next to Dehan and handed her the album. "There, that's him. Was he hot or what?" She wheezed. Dehan studied the photos without expression. May went on, nudging Dehan with her elbow. "'Course, he'd be forty now, a bit too old for you, hey?"

Dehan handed me the album and I looked at a large photograph of about fifteen people against a backdrop of pine trees in what appeared to be a mountainous area. Most of the people there were young men and women, probably in their early to midtwenties, though behind them there was an older man, perhaps in his late thirties. He was the only one who was not smiling. His gaze was more what you might describe as keen. Next to him was a woman, maybe ten years younger than him. She looked Asian, perhaps Filipina. May was saying, "Danny is

FIRE FROM HEAVEN | 13

the one in the middle, sitting at the front, with the open denim shirt."

I found him. He was a handsome young man with a mischievous grin and floppy brown hair. Hunkered down on his left was a powerfully built, dark-haired guy with his arm around Danny's shoulders, and on his right was a pretty girl, laughing, with her head on his shoulder. Danny's arms were both on his knees. I looked up at Stuart, who was watching me carefully.

"May I take a copy of this?"

He gestured at me with an open hand. "Be our guest."

I took a picture on my cell, then showed Stuart the album. "Who are the two either side of him?"

He took it and set it on his lap, gazed at it for a while with sad eyes. "This was their first field trip after he'd joined them. The man standing at the back is Donald Kirkpatrick, a highly intelligent man. Some kind of scientist by training. He founded the group. The two at the front . . ." He took a deep breath, which turned into a sigh. "I remember them, I don't recall their names. May?"

He handed it to her. She glanced but didn't take it. "Paul Estevez and Jane Harrison."

"They look pretty close."

"I told you, everybody loved him, but he was a free spirit. For them it was probably nothing more than a social activity. For him it was a search for the truth. And, as Donald points out, it was a search that cost him his life." She regarded me with an expression that was close to pity. It was only the hint of contempt that stopped it getting there. "Really, Detective, you are asking the wrong questions. What you need to be asking is, what did he discover? What did he unearth that made him a target?"

I spread my hands. "Okay. Tell me. What *did* he discover that made him a target?"

Dehan was watching May with the kind of expressionless face she normally reserved for people she wanted to slap. Before May could answer me, Dehan asked, "A target for whom, Mrs. Brown?

And also, what evidence have you got that he *was* a target for somebody? If you have that evidence, why have you not shared it with the police?"

Stuart had raised his hands in a "slow down" gesture and was smiling at the coffee table. "Hang on, hang on, let's take these questions one at a time. First: we are not withholding any information. Second: we do not have any proof, as you would understand it, that Danny was anybody's target." He spread his hands and nodded. "Beyond the obvious fact that he *was* murdered. Third: we don't know who he was a target for, any more than a herd of gazelles in Africa knows who is shooting at them from the helicopter. However, we are satisfied, based on the evidence we have, which is the same evidence that you have, that Danny was not killed by a human being." He shrugged his shoulders and shook his head in an oddly helpless gesture. "It simply isn't possible." He gazed at me a moment. "And to answer your question, Detective Stone, we don't know what he had unearthed."

"But you think he had unearthed something."

It was May who answered. "Stuart is not convinced, but I am. He would often go off for several days at a time. Sometimes alone, sometimes with members of the group; sometimes it was for a night, sometimes several days at a time. He never told us what he was doing or where he was going. That's why we didn't raise the alarm that weekend. *I* think he discovered something..."

Stuart sighed and attempted a smile. "It will sound absurd to you, Detectives. It seems absurd to anyone who has not done the research. But there are very eminent people, in the White House, in the Pentagon, in academia, all of whom are agreed that there *is* a conspiracy to conceal the truth about UFOs. And we think it is possible, May is convinced, that Danny had found something. And whatever it was he found got him killed." Again he shrugged, again he spread his hands in that helpless gesture. "Nobody else had a motive. Nobody else had the *means*!"

I thought about it for a long moment. I was aware of Dehan watching me. Maybe she wanted to slap me too. I pointed at the album, which lay open on the coffee table. "Have you got contact details for Paul and Jane?"

May shook her head. "No, but Donald will have." She reached down by the side of the sofa and picked up a brown leather handbag. From it she extracted a small notepad and a pen. She scrawled an address and a phone number and handed it to Dehan. "He'll be happy to see you."

Dehan took it and thanked her. "One last question before we go. Can you tell us about his movements that night?"

May shook her head. "No. We last saw him on the Friday. They were all going on some kind of field trip, after which they were going to have a party or something at Donald's place. We never saw him again."

We thanked them and stood. They followed us to the door. As Stuart opened it, he held my eye a moment. "The FBI tried to silence us, you know."

I frowned.

Dehan snapped, "The FBI tried to silence you? How?"

He nodded. "They called on the telephone and they came to see us: two men. They'll deny it, of course. But they came and advised us, for our own good, to keep quiet. Don't be surprised if you hear from them. They'll tell you to drop the investigation and close the case."

We thanked them again and stepped out into the midday glare.

THREE

We didn't get into the car; instead I walked to the top of Beach Avenue and looked down. Dehan was sitting on the hood of my old, burgundy Jag, watching me. I pointed. "Soundview Park is four or five hundred yards down there. That's where they found him. What do you say we go and have a look?"

She nodded, stood, and followed me. We walked in silence for a while, enjoying the sunshine and the warmth. After a moment, she slipped her arm through mine and leaned against me as she walked.

"Are you buying this alien . . ."

"Don't say BS."

She glanced at me. "So you are buying it?"

"That is a very open question, Dehan."

"What do you mean? It's a yes or no question. Are you buying it? Yes, I am; no, I'm not."

I raised an eyebrow at her, but she looked away, as though she was checking for traffic on an empty road. We crossed Patterson Avenue and continued down Beach toward the park, which was now clearly visible at the end of the road, about a hundred yards away.

"Okay," I said, "what is 'it' exactly? What is it, precisely, you are asking me if I am buying? Are you asking me if I believe that alien life exists on other planets, or moons? If so, I don't believe it, I think it is impossible that it does *not* exist. Are you asking me if I believe alien life forms are visiting Earth? I just don't know, but I know there are some very smart people who do. Or are you asking me whether I believe that Danny was murdered by an extraterrestrial?"

"That one."

"Then the answer is, I don't know who killed him, yet. Statistically he is more likely to have been killed by a human being, over sex or money. But I am not going to make the evidence fit my theory, I am going to develop my theory..."

"Based on the evidence, yadda yadda. I know. But come on, Stone! He was shot by an alien with a ray gun? Seriously? And while we chase little green men, the killer pisses his pants laughing and gets away with murder."

We had reached the bend in the road where it becomes O'Brien Avenue. To our right there was an untended wilderness of knee-high grass and flowers interspersed with oak and linden trees. I stopped and she stopped with me. I gazed at it a moment and said absently, "This is what the world *should* look like, Dehan."

She looked at me in surprise and smiled. "Why, John, you're a romantic after all!"

I smiled back and pointed in among the undergrowth. "He was found in there."

We picked our way through a broad border of grasses, wildflowers, and bindweed until we came to a broad expanse of coarse scrub and gray clay, bounded by a path that entered the park from the west, ran along the riverbank for two hundred yards, and then turned north, skirting the amphitheater. I stopped and looked around for a moment, remembering the photos I'd studied. Then I pointed south, to a slight rise where I could see a small tree. "Over there, by that oak tree."

We trudged across the dense, cloying soil for maybe a hundred yards, until we came to a tall, spindly pin oak which twenty years earlier would have been little more than the sapling I had seen in the picture. I stood by the tree and took ten paces to the west, turned, and looked at Dehan, who was watching me with her hands in her back pockets. "This is the spot," I said. "Try to visualize it. Sometime on Sunday night. It's been raining on and off since late afternoon. It's dark. His feet, in his thongs, are here." I found two large clumps of clay and positioned them where his feet had been. "Facing out toward the water. His body, or what is left of it, is lying back from his feet. Imagine," I said, "that a guy with a samurai sword, as sharp as a scalpel, had cut through his ankles, and he had fallen straight back."

"Wait."

She picked up a stick and came over, scratched out the shape of his body, with no head, lying on the ground, with his arms at forty-five-degree angles from his body. Then she went and found a large clump of clay, the size of a melon. "His head is . . ." She gauged the distance with her eye and placed the lump where his head had been found. ". . . about here. And . . ." She grinned, found a twig and two acorns, and placed them where his genitals would have been. ". . . the pièce de résistance!"

I pointed at the ground. "This is clay. It sucks up water, holds it a long time, and keeps its shape."

She nodded. "I hear you. There should have been footprints." She screwed up her face like an angry fist. "But wait, please, let's not get ahead of ourselves, Sensei. Let's look at each step separately and then see if we can fit them together at the end. First, of the people we know of, who had anything like a possible motive?"

I scratched my head. "Anything *like* a possible motive? Any one of them, Dehan. We just don't know anything about his relationships yet. He was attractive, single, wanting to stay unattached. Right there you have a breeding ground for motives: jealousy, rejection, envy . . ."

"Okay, so opportunity." She sighed and corrected herself. "Okay, not opportunity, because we know nothing of his movements, so any one of them might have had opportunity, including his parents."

I nodded. "Which brings us to means."

We stared at each other for a long time. Then she threw her hands in the air and expostulated, "Son of a gun! Means! Sure, anyone with a laser scalpel in 1998! But not just a laser scalpel—a laser scalpel capable of incinerating an entire body at the same time as surgically removing the head, the feet, and the . . ." She sighed. "This is bullshit, Stone." She turned to me. "He was not killed by aliens!"

I chuckled in a way I knew was annoying. "It's not just the scalpel and the incineration, there is also the question of how the killer got here across the wet clay and then left, without leaving any tracks. Even if we argue that Danny might have been killed somewhere else and deposited here, the killer still has to cross the wet clay and lay out the feet, the head . . ." I shook my head. "And then go back. It's a hell of an undertaking."

She made a three-hundred-and-sixty-degree turn, scanning the entire visible park and the river. Then shook her head. I pointed up at the sky. "The lights were seen up there." She stared at me like she was about to smack me. "Don't look at me in that tone of voice, Dehan. The lights were seen by several hundred witnesses, they are a part of the evidence we have to sift through. Suck it up, baby. They were seen directly above the scene, firing lasers down toward the ground. They then moved south for a way and suddenly vanished in a flash of white light."

She turned and pointed at me. "Okay, Stone, I'm going to come at this from a different angle."

"Good."

"Forget the whole UFO thing, right?"

"This is different?"

"Let's face it, if he was killed by an alien, we will never prove it and, as you pointed out to May Brown, we have no extradition treaty with Betelgeuse, so we will never catch him. Therefore the only line of inquiry worth pursuing is, the killer was human."

I shrugged. "The statistics are on your side, at least."

"Shut up and tell me what you think: our killer is smart, he thinks out of the box. He would have to, to come up with a plan like this *and* get away with it. I mean . . ." She gave a small laugh. "If you hadn't pissed off Captain Jennifer Cuevas back in the day, we would never have been assigned to cold cases, and he would have got away with this. And he still might! So he is smart, and an original thinker."

"Can't argue with that."

"And . . ." She raised a finger. "He is daring. He is not afraid to go extreme and take risks."

I raised an eyebrow at her. "Hmmm . . ."

"So, he puts together a drone, or whatever equivalent they had back in the '90s, with all the flashing lights and lasers. He hovers it over the park. It's daring because it is drawing everybody's attention, but it is clever because it also pretty much guarantees that nobody is going to come into the park. Remember, in 1998 *The X-Files* is at the peak of its popularity, as is abduction syndrome. So people are *scared*!"

I made a "you have a point" face and nodded.

She went on, "So then, and this is the really daring bit, he comes in off the river on a hovercraft."

I smiled. "A what?"

"Like the ones they use in the swamps in Florida. If anybody hears the noise they'll think it's the UFO. He positions the body, takes off back into the sound, brings the drone in to land on the craft, and makes off across the river to . . . what? Powell Cove? Little Neck, Kings Point, wherever!"

"It's certainly daring."

"Is it less likely than aliens? Have you got a better theory that doesn't involve *Predator*?"

I shook my head. "I have no theories at all at the moment." I pointed down toward the water. "You have a line of trees between the park and the river. Your hovercraft would have to break through them."

She nodded. "Yes, but over there, down by Harding Park, you have a little harbor with no trees, and he would have access through there."

"That's true." I thought a little more. She danced around with her fists up, like Cassius Clay or Bruce Lee. "C'mon, Stone. Hit me. Show me whatcha got."

"How did he lay out the body without leaving any prints in the mud?"

She thought for a moment. "He settled the hovercraft on the mud, and placed his victim without getting down, lying on his belly on the craft, and then left."

I nodded for a while, visualizing it, then said, "You about ready for lunch?" She nodded vigorously and we turned and started walking back toward Beach Avenue. I said, "It's very good. In fact, I only see two problems with your ingenious scenario, Dehan."

"What?"

"The first is, you are assuming he was killed elsewhere, but you still leave unanswered the question, how did he kill him? The second, and more difficult, is, having laid the corpse out and sprinkled the ash in the form of the body, on leaving, the very powerful fan that the hovercraft uses to move about would have blown that ash all over the park, even wet."

She stopped dead in her tracks and sighed. "Damn it! I should have seen that." She started to walk again. "It does tell us one thing, though. Danny was killed—or the body was placed—after the worst of the rain, because heavy rain would have washed the ash away."

"Yup. That's true. Now we just need a hovercraft that doesn't use a powerful fan."

She shoved her hands in her pockets and eyed me. "You mean like a flying saucer with a dilithium crystal warp drive."

"Don't be downhearted, Dehan. Top of our to-do list, after we've talked to everyone: make a list of vehicles that could have covered that distance, discreetly, and deposited the body without leaving tracks."

"Yeah, makes sense. Also, a list of tools or instruments that could have generated that kind of intense, focused heat over an area of, what, five and a half feet? To cut off his ankles and his head."

I looked at her, chewing my lip as we walked, turning over what she'd said in my head. I knew for a fact that there was no such instrument or weapon. It just didn't exist in terrestrial technology. But I didn't say so.

We came out of the park and made our way up toward my ancient, uncomputerized, primitive brute of a car. There was not a shred of software in it. Even the lock was mechanical. As I slipped the key in the door and opened it, I found that oddly comforting.

Before getting in, I leaned on the roof to look at Dehan, and felt the heat through my sleeve. She leaned on the other side and lifted her sunglasses to squint at me. I said, "Hamburger, beer, Donald Kirkpatrick."

She blinked. "The elegance of your syntax is matched only by the beauty of your words, Sensei."

"I thought so," I said, and climbed in behind the old walnut steering wheel.

FOUR

Just where Soundview Avenue meets White Plains Road, there is a cute bar and grill called Maravillas. It serves Latin American food that is superb, in a setting you just wouldn't expect. We ate in silence, partly because the food was so good and partly because Dehan didn't want to discuss the case. When we had drained our beers and paid, we left the car by the restaurant and walked the short distance to Pugsley Avenue.

Pugsley Avenue is a cul-de-sac that abuts Pugsley Creek Park, and Donald Kirkpatrick's house was the last on the right, before the footpath that leads to the park. It was a big, quirky, white clapboard affair standing apart from the other houses in the street, in its own grounds. It was on two stories, plus an attic and a basement, and had six stone steps leading up to the front door, with wrought iron railings on either side. The garden was untended, and the fence and gate, rather than white picket, were steel tubing and wire mesh, like Ochoa's.

We pushed through, followed the concrete path past a huge cypress tree with a wooden bench under it, and climbed the concrete steps. After I'd rung the bell, the door was eventually opened by a woman I recognized. She was now in her late forties, but she had aged well and was still recognizable as the Asian-looking woman who was standing next to Donald in the photograph we had seen.

"Mrs. Kirkpatrick?" She nodded and I showed her my badge. "I'm Detective John Stone. This is my partner, Detective Dehan. Is your husband in?"

Anxiety momentarily contracted her face, but there was a kind of obstinate strength in her eyes. She said, "Yes. But he's in his den. He's busy."

"May we come in? We won't take much of your time. We just need to talk to him for a minute."

She backed away a step, which I took, rightly or wrongly, as an invitation to come in. I stepped over the threshold into a broad entrance hall, and Dehan came in behind me. Mrs. Kirkpatrick backed up some more, saying, "Umm . . ." and Dehan closed the door.

She didn't look happy. "Okay, I'll go and tell him. Wait, please . . ."

I watched her disappear toward the kitchen and wondered absently what had turned her into an obedient, servile woman. My gut told me it didn't come naturally. I dismissed the thought and looked around. On my right a door stood open onto a large, comfortable living room. The furniture looked expensive, but old and threadbare. There were bookcases in every available space, and even so there were more books than they could hold. So they stood in small piles everywhere you looked, in front of other books, on the floor, on the sideboard.

Ahead, a staircase rose straight to the next floor. The banister was painted white, and the carpet was an ugly dark green. Past the stairs, on the left, I could see light streaming in from the kitchen. There was a smell of baking bread, and I could hear feet stomping up wooden stairs, and a nagging male voice explaining to Mrs. Kirkpatrick the million and one ways in which she had failed him —yet again. I told myself I had probably found the answer to my question about her servility.

His shadow loomed across the light and then Donald Kirkpatrick moved down the passage toward us. He was at least six foot six, slim and stooped. His knees had an odd trick of poking out to the sides as he walked. His face should have been handsome, but his irritable bad temper had etched it with ugly lines.

"Is it too much to ask that the New York Police Department phone before just turning up? We do have lives, you know, and jobs."

He was drawing breath to follow up on his greeting, so I cut him short. "Yes. I'm sorry. Crime waits for no man," I added facetiously and smiled. "We won't take up much of your time, Mr. Kirkpatrick. It's about Danny Brown. You do remember him?"

His thick eyebrows, which were turning a snowy white, knitted over his long nose. "Of course I remember him. What can you possibly want with Danny after twenty years?"

I stared at him without expression for a slow count of five, then said, "May we come in and perhaps sit down? It will make it easier to explain. We are not here to inconvenience anybody, Mr. Kirkpatrick, we are only trying to solve a homicide."

He sighed noisily and gracelessly and flung a long arm in the direction of the living room. "Very well. Of course. We may as well have coffee. Jasmine, make coffee. And *try* not to make it too strong this time." He walked ahead of us through the door, muttering, "I've only been telling her for twenty years."

He lowered himself into an old, cracked Chesterfield. Beside it there was a small table with a large ashtray and a pipe settled in it. Dehan sat on the sofa, and I took the chair directly across from him. He began scraping out his pipe with a small penknife and spoke without looking up.

"Well, what do you want to know?"

"We'd like you to talk us through the last forty-eight hours of Danny's life."

He stopped scraping and stared at me incredulously. Then he stared at Dehan, then back at me. "You have got to be joking. What is this? Is this some kind of joke?"

I sighed. "No, Mr. Kirkpatrick. Believe it or not, the NYPD does not tend to joke about murder. We run a cold-cases unit out of the Forty-Third Precinct, and we are reviewing Danny's case."

He shook his head and went back to scraping the bowl of his pipe. "Priceless. This is priceless. You ignore the case for twenty years and now you want to open it up again and find the . . ."

My patience ran out. I snapped, "Mr. Kirkpatrick, I am as unimpressed by your opinion as I am by your lack of good manners. Now, we can do this here or we can do it down at the station house. Wherever we do it, we'll get done faster if you spare us all your opinions on things you know nothing about." His eyes bulged and his face went scarlet. He looked like he was about to rupture an artery, so I said, "I believe Danny came to see you on the Friday. You and the group were going on some kind of field trip, is that correct?"

He sat working his jaw. Dehan said, "Sir, it is probably simplest just to answer our questions, then we can get out of your hair. Did Danny come over on the Friday?"

"To answer your *impertinent* question, Danny and some ten or eleven other people came over to my house on that Friday. Friday the fifth of June. We then got into three off-road vehicles, two Jeeps and a Land Rover, and drove to Macomb Mountain. There we camped for the night and attempted to make contact with the Visitors. Does that answer your question?"

Dehan said, "When you say 'the Visitors,' you mean . . . ?"

"Yes, Detective, and you can mock me to your heart's content. Believe me, I have been mocked by brighter people than yourself and I have become impervious! Aliens, extraterrestrials, ETs, trans-dimensional travelers! Whatever you want to call them. We attempted to contact them!"

I frowned at him. "Did you succeed?"

He looked surprised. He searched my face for any indication of mockery. He didn't find any because I was not mocking. After a moment, he shrugged. "Maybe."

I thought for a moment. "What is it, exactly, that makes you unsure?"

He tapped the scrapings from the bowl of his pipe and began to pack it with tobacco. Without looking up from what he was doing, he said, "Your partner has no time for what she regards as an absurdity, but I take it you are open to the possibility that beings that are not originally from Earth walk among us, or at least visit us from time to time."

I nodded. "I am certainly open to that possibility. And I think you'll find my partner is not as closed to the idea as she appears to be."

He seemed not to have heard. He put the pipe in his mouth and lit it with two tapers, sending big billows of sweet-smelling smoke drifting across the room. Dehan glanced at me, but I could not make out her expression. It might have been withering. Kirkpatrick started to speak again.

"If you try to imagine a mountain wolf trying to communicate with a human being . . ." He paused. "You are nowhere near *close* to the difficulty a human being has trying to communicate with an alien civilization. Because at least the two species of mammals have common DNA, common instincts, broadly speaking a common environment, even common basic values. There are, for example, basic body movements that all mammals will understand, so there is a common, basic framework on which to build some form of communication.

"But when we try to communicate with the Visitors, it is more akin to trying to communicate with water, or air, or an amoeba. I am not talking about the disparity in intelligence, I am talking about the *alien nature of their form of intelligence*." He labored each word with a downward stroke of his pipe. "We have no common points of reference on which to start to build a system of communication . . ."

"In that case," I said, "perhaps I should ask you, what makes you think you might have?" He glanced at me. I explained,

"Established communication. What makes you think you might have?"

He nodded. "That would be a better question." He took a moment, gazing into the incandescent bowl of his pipe, as though my improved question were in there, smoldering nicely. "Stone, I am a scientist by trade and by training. That means that my brain is conditioned to do two things: prove by experimentation, and *evaluate the weight—the validity—of the evidence!*"

He spat the last words furiously. For a moment he looked to me like a man fighting back against a lifetime of unfounded, damaging criticism. He leaned back in his chair and went on.

"Whatever you may think, I have no time, no patience, for charlatans and fools who invent evidence where they can't find any. Telepathy *has not* been proven! Some, unrepeated, unduplicated, experiments have indicated that perhaps, at a very short distance in space, there may be some quantum-level influence of one brain on another! That is not the same—*not the same*—as telepathy."

Dehan gave a small cough. "Forgive me, Mr. Kirkpatrick, I am not following you. What has telepathy got to do with..."

He scowled at her. "It seems that the Visitors employ some form of brain-to-brain communication. And I am trying to impress upon you that I, as a scientist, am very, *very* resistant to this idea. I do not accept the existence of ESP, astral projection, or any of this other New Age hippie garbage that so-called researchers go in for these days. I am a *scientist!*" He paused for a long moment, puffing and sending aromatic clouds across the room. "However, on that night, it is possible that we might have received some form of brain-to-brain communication."

Dehan turned to me. "Is this relevant to our investigation, Stone?"

I smiled blandly at her. "Let's find out." I turned to Kirkpatrick. "I know Princeton has been conducting experiments for over twenty years on how consciousness interacts with the physical world at a quantum level. But I understood that the electrical fields generated by the brain were so weak..."

He interrupted me. "That is precisely the point. The brain generates fields at the quantum level, and they are miniscule. So communication between one and another is practically impossible, even when the heads are touching. However..." He sighed. He looked almost like a man about to make a guilty admission. "The issue is not, in fact, the strength or weakness of the signal. A very feeble receptor is capable of capturing a single quantum particle, an electron or a photon, over millions of light-years' distance!"

Dehan snorted. "Come on! That's ridiculous! How would you even prove such a thing?"

I smiled at her, impressed not for the first time by her irreverence and total lack of respect for her supposed superiors. Kirkpatrick flushed and glared at her. She shrugged and spread her hands. "Sorry, but really..."

Dehan has a face it is hard to stay mad at, and Kirkpatrick sighed and shook his head. "Tonight, Detective Dehan, do yourself a favor and step outside. Try to find a place where the damned city lights have not flooded the sky, maybe Soundview Park, or take a drive to Long Island. Look up at the sky and pick the smallest star you can find and stare at it. When you do that, remind yourself that the feeble electrical fields in your brain are capturing and processing photons that were projected *millions* of years ago, by a star millions of light-years away."

Her eyebrows rode up her forehead and her jaw sagged just a little. "Son of a gun!"

"The problem," he went on, "is not whether a comparatively feeble instrument is capable of capturing the signal. The problem is interference. Which is why during the day, or in the heart of Manhattan, you will not capture that same photon."

I nodded. "I understand. So what happened on Macomb Mountain?"

We heard a noise outside the door. I rose and opened it, and Jasmine came in carrying a tray with a coffeepot, a jug of milk, sugar, and four cups. She set the tray down and began to serve us coffee. I sat again and looked at Kirkpatrick, who was watching his wife intently. I said, "What happened, Mr. Kirkpatrick?"

His eyes swiveled back to me, and he said, savagely, "Jasmine received a brain-to-brain communication from the Visitors."

FIVE

A LOT OF THOUGHTS FLASHED THROUGH MY MIND IN that moment. I logged them and watched Jasmine with interest as she sat next to Dehan and sipped her coffee. I wondered if he would let her tell her own story, but I was pretty sure he wouldn't, and he didn't.

"We had a radio which we had adapted to transmit and receive signals on a very wide range of frequencies. We also had visual scanners which were capable of picking up both high and low frequencies of light beyond the visual range in the night sky. Macomb Mountain, where we were, near the peak, affords a spectacular view of the heavens, and we were able to see and pick up a number of phenomena. A lot of it was suggestive, some of it was highly suggestive, none of it was conclusive."

Dehan failed to suppress a sigh. "Could you tell us about . . ."

"I'm coming to that! It was about two in the morning. The fire had started to burn low, and a number of people had withdrawn to their tents. There were half a dozen of us who were still talking about what we had seen: lights moving across the sky, doing right-angle turns, turning back on themselves at speeds of several thousand miles an hour . . ." He dismissed these things with a wave of his hand. "The usual stuff."

I asked, "Who remained after the others had retired?"

He sighed. "Uh . . . Danny—he was inexhaustible, and deeply committed—Dixon, Rafael, Paul, Jane, and myself."

Jasmine spoke for the first time. Her voice was small, but, like her eyes, it carried a strength that suggested stubbornness, even obstinacy. She said, "I was also there, Donald. That is how you know I went into the trance."

He stared hard at his pipe for a moment. I could see his jaw muscle going. "Clearly," he said at last. "Jasmine was also there. She had been sitting in her sleeping bag. At about ten past two, she lay down. At about twelve minutes past, she began to tremble, moving her arms and her feet up and down in jerky movements. Then she began to speak. I remember it vividly. At first she made inarticulate noises, mainly vowels, but then she suddenly spoke, and said, 'We have chosen you for communication. Jasmine is our channel for the simplicity of her mind. Daniel is our actor for his energy. He will spread our message. Donald is the rock on which we build. Dixon, Paul, Jane, you shall make paths for others to tread.'"

He stopped abruptly. I became aware of an old grandfather clock against one wall. Its ticking seemed surprisingly loud. Through the front window, I saw a woman talking silently to a postman. The midday light seemed to glare through the net curtains.

Jasmine said, "That is not all the message said."

Dehan turned to her and studied her for a moment. "What else did it say?"

She looked at her husband, and I was astonished to see real affection in her face. He scowled down at his pipe. She gazed at him, smiling while she spoke.

"I believe Donald saved my life that night. Because the message went on, 'Daniel and Jasmine, follow the path to the glade now, for direct contact, to meet with us.'" She turned to Dehan. "But Donald would not let me go. The glade was half a mile away, through the forest. He forbade it. I think if we had

FIRE FROM HEAVEN | 33

gone, they would have killed us both, as they later killed Danny."

"So did Danny go?"

She shook her head. "No, Donald stopped us. He knew it was not safe. Danny said if Donald didn't want us to go, he would not go."

I scratched my chin, turning the events over in my mind, trying to visualize them. I asked her, "What was it like?"

She frowned at the carpet, like she was wondering where the voice had come from.

I said, "Receiving the message: What was it like? What did it feel like?"

She looked at Donald, who ignored her. Finally, she turned to me and said, "It was strange. It was as though my own thoughts had taken on a life of their own. As though invisible hands were moving my thoughts. And then, when I began to speak, it was as though my own will had been cancelled, and my mouth was speaking on its own. I had no control over what it was saying."

"You were not aware of the presence of thoughts in your mind that were not your own?"

The thought seemed to be something new to her. She frowned and after a moment shook her head. "No, nothing like that."

I nodded. "This was Friday night?"

Kirkpatrick nodded and stood. "That was Friday night. Early Saturday morning we returned." He walked over to a bookcase located behind my back and returned with two paperbacks. He handed one to me and one to Dehan. "*Heaven's Fire*. Everything is recounted there faithfully from the notes I took at the time. I don't think there is much more we can tell you."

I took it and examined it. The dedication read: *This book is dedicated to my friend and colleague, Daniel Brown, whose destiny it was to spread the message.*

"Thank you. There is just one more thing. I believe there was a party on Saturday . . ."

He snorted. "Hardly. We were all tired. We had a few drinks, discussed what had happened—or not happened—Paul and Dixon were a little disgruntled, I think, that I had forbidden Jasmine from going to the glade. Everybody went home. That was it."

Dehan said, "Except that Danny next showed up in Soundview Park, dead."

He knocked the smoldering ash from his pipe into his ashtray. "Quite so. I can only say that I am glad, whatever the others may say, that I stopped Jasmine from going." He shook his head and gestured at the two paperbacks. "Everything else is in your books. I suggest you read them, and if you have any more questions after that, you are welcome to phone me, make an appointment, and come and see me."

I studied his face a moment. He met my eye. I nodded and turned to Dehan, making a question with my face. She shook her head and said, "I have no more questions."

"Then we shall leave you to your work." I stood. "Thank you for your time and for the books. You have been very helpful." I turned to his wife. "Jasmine."

She looked at the floor, and Kirkpatrick rose and led us to the front door. There I stopped and said, "Paul Estevez and Jane Harrison. Have you got contact information for them?"

He pulled a pen from his pocket and made a note on the back of one of his own business cards. "We lost touch with Jane. This is Paul's address and phone number. He's not far, up Soundview Avenue. He runs some form of martial arts school. He's become a little disillusioned, like all of us, I suppose." He hesitated a moment, then said, "The day after tomorrow, there's a small conference at the Marriott, on Bassett Avenue, near the hospital. There will be a hundred people or so, perhaps a little less. We have a very distinguished speaker coming. He'll be discussing the intentions of the Visitors, whether they are friendly or hostile, whether they have killed before. You may be interested." He reached over to a small table by an umbrella stand and picked up a couple of leaflets. "Come along as my guests."

We thanked him again, and he let us out into the early-afternoon glare. As we strolled down toward Gildersleeve Avenue, on our way back to Maravillas, I thrust my hands deep into my pockets, took a deep breath, and asked, "Impressions? Thoughts?"

She stared up at the perfect blue sky. "It's not the distance stopping me from seeing the stars, but the interference." She matched my sigh with one of her own. "I don't know, Stone. He is a very believable witness. So is she. If they were telling me any other story, I would be inclined to believe them." She shrugged. "Maybe I am just a narrow-minded, bigoted cop, but it's going to take a lot more than their testimony to convince me that Danny Brown was shot by an alien with a ray gun."

I didn't answer, and we walked on in silence. The street was empty and quiet but for the lazy, midday song of the birds in the nearby park and the buzz of an occasional bee. After a while she added, "I'll say this though. I am pretty sure that *they* believe their testimony."

I looked at her and thought about it. "You may be right."

She ignored me and went on, "They go up to this very remote place, at night. They are surrounded by . . ." She shook her head. "What is it, six million acres of dense forest. The daily bread of these people is *The X-Files*, *Close Encounters*, Roswell, and the infinite number of books that have been written on the subject of UFOs, aliens, and the men in black. They see, or persuade themselves that they have seen, the strange phenomena in the sky, and then they sit around the campfire and start talking, building themselves up into a state of high suggestibility. Right?"

"Okay."

We turned into Gildersleeve and started walking toward White Plains Road. Dehan shrugged, half nodding and half apologizing for what she was about to say. "Now, Jasmine is very sweet and nice, but she is also servile and obedient and, let's be honest,

Stone, a bit simple. I'm not saying she's stupid, but she isn't exactly a soaring intellect either."

"Granted. On both counts."

"So some deep unconscious desire kicks in and she puts herself into a trance." She stopped dead, turned to face me, and poked me in the chest with her finger. "Listen! She has an internal conflict. She has been conditioned since she was a kid to be servile and obedient to her father. But she also has a craving, a need, to be special for him. She knows that Kirkpatrick admires Danny, so her unconscious mind creates a fantasy, which she plays out as a trance induced by the aliens, who have selected her and Danny to be their chosen messengers, while her husband is elevated to the position of patriarch—the rock on which they build. Which is a direct borrowing from the Bible, by the way."

I stared at her. "Wow, that is pretty deep, Dehan. It would take some confirming, but my gut says you may be onto something. It rings true. Even if you are assuming a lot and also straying out of our field a little."

She shrugged and turned, and we carried on walking. "Screw fields. We go where we need to go, right? But what it doesn't do is get us any closer to who *did* kill Danny."

"Perhaps."

"What do you mean, perhaps?"

"I am being cryptic. It is my prerogative as Holmes to your Watson."

"Screw you, Sherlock. You know I'm right."

We rounded the corner into White Plains and started toward the fork in the road. I could see my Jaguar parked facing us and allowed myself a moment of sentimental pleasure. It was a magnificent beast in an elegant, understated burgundy, a Mark II from 1964, with 210 bhp. It was beautiful, both elegant and powerful, the way a car should be. But, it struck me, it was not the power or the elegance that I loved, but the simplicity. It was old-fashioned, mechanical, simple.

Dehan took hold of my arm. "Like you, my friend," she said, and I realized I had been thinking aloud.

I gave a small, humorless laugh. "Like Stuart said, this is the dawning of the Age of Aquarius. Perhaps Jennifer Cuevas was right. Perhaps I do belong to a bygone age. Perhaps I have lost my relevance. Perhaps, Dehan, we are entering an age when aliens murder humans. Perhaps the race riots of the future will be between humans and aliens, and the hated color will not be black or brown or white, but green."

She was silent for a while, then she smiled fondly at me and asked, "Do you know what my father would have called you?"

"A dreamer? A visionary? A man ahead of his time?"

She shook her head. "Uh-uh, a schmuck."

I unlocked the door, not with a button but with a key, climbed into the leather seat behind the wooden wheel, and shoved that same key in the ignition. I turned that key and gunned the engine, and sat for a moment listening to the satisfying rumble, visualizing Danny, standing on that grassy knoll, looking out over the vast, dark East River, watching those lights flashing in the sky, with those lasers shooting down at him out of the sky, out of the dark clouds and the rain. Did I believe it? I turned to Dehan.

"Fire from Heaven. Three hundred years ago, they would have said it was an angel or a demon that had struck him down."

She nodded. "A different age. A different kind of myth."

I nodded back. "Or a different kind of explanation."

SIX

Dehan dialed, waited a moment, and said, "Paul Estevez . . . ? Good afternoon, this is Detective Carmen Dehan of the NYPD. I was wondering if you could spare some time to see us this afternoon . . . ? Yeah, it's about Danny Brown . . . Uh-huh, a long time, I know. We could come to you. We can be there in twenty minutes . . . Thank you. Appreciate it." She hung up. "He can give us half an hour before his first class."

"Good."

I put the beast in gear, pulled out into the traffic, and headed up Soundview Avenue at a slow cruise. Dehan checked her watch. "What do you say we talk to Paul, pick up some groceries, and head on back . . ." She looked at me sidelong with a stupid, sheepish grin on her face and started laughing.

It was contagious. I laughed back. "What?"

She turned and looked out the window, pinching the bridge of her nose and still laughing. "I dunno, Stone. It's stupid. It's just . . ."

"What, Dehan? Say it."

"I was going to say, 'head home.' It just sounds so weird to me."

"You don't like it? You know my house is your home. *Mi casa es tu casa*, right?"

She blushed like a teenager. "Yeah, I know. No, I do like it. It's good. It just feels weird."

I was still smiling. "So we get some groceries and go home..."

She spent the next minute laughing like a fifteen-year-old and she finally said, "Yeah . . . and we go through everything over a glass of wine or two."

I nodded. "What, and we don't put in an appearance at the station today?"

She shrugged. "What for?"

"When was the last time you were at the station?"

"What are you, my boss now?" She was still smiling, but there was an edge to her voice.

"You know I'm not. I'm just curious. In all the time I've known you, you have never once not set foot in the station."

She shrugged. "So what? Back then I was trying to prove something."

I eyed her sidelong for a bit and she stared straight ahead, with her face concealed behind her shades.

Finally, I said, "Can I tell you what I think?"

"No."

"I think you are worried about how Mo and Maria—and the whole damn precinct—is going to react if they find out we are . . ."

I gestured, searching for the word. She turned and stared at me, repressing what seemed to be involuntary, nervous laughter. "Don't tell me the great John Stone is suddenly lost for words! Find out we are *what*?"

I shook my head, feeling oddly embarrassed. "Sixty-five million years ago, when I was young and the dinosaurs walked the Earth, people like me would have said, 'an item,' 'going out,' 'a couple,' or even 'boyfriend and girlfriend.' But nowadays terms like that can be a minefield."

"Bullshit." She said it without anger. "You just don't know

what to call us. Don't worry, I don't either." She shrugged. "Maybe that's why I don't want to..."

I nodded. "I hear you."

She frowned, suddenly anxious. "I didn't offend you? I didn't mean..."

I smiled and tried to look like I meant it. "Of course not. It's cool. We're learning as we go. Groceries and review... at home."

She grinned. "Cool."

"But tomorrow we go back to the desk. Or the inspector is going to want to know why. And so are Mo and his pals. The longer we leave it, the worse it gets."

Paul's gym was on the corner of Randall and Rosedale, in a run-down shopping mall by the gardens there. We were ten minutes early, but we found him in a small office in his dojo, dressed in his dobok, sitting behind a desk under a Korean flag. He was going through his books and stood and smiled as we walked in. He pulled up a couple of chairs for us. And as we sat, he glanced at the clock on the wall.

"I don't mean to be discourteous, but my class starts in forty minutes. I am always drumming into my pupils the need to be punctual, and also the importance of commitment. So..." He spread his hands. "I must be as good as my word. This kind of thing is really important in this kind of neighborhood."

I agreed and told him so with my face. "If there were more teachers with that kind of attitude, we would probably be out of a job. I doubt we'll keep you that long, Mr. Estevez. We just want to ask you a couple of questions about Danny."

He leaned back in his chair, took a deep breath, and shook his head. "I don't know what I can tell you. You spoke to Don? He's said just about everything there is to say about it."

Dehan said, "You believe, like him, that Danny was killed by an extraterrestrial?"

He shrugged. "I know it sounds crazy, but any other explanation is even crazier. Plus..." He shrugged and shook his head again. "You had to be there, man."

I said, "You were there on the Friday night . . ."

"On Macomb Mountain? Yeah, I was there. That was weird, man. It was . . ." He laughed. "That was fucked up."

"In what way, exactly?"

He put two massive fists on the desk in front of him and seemed to study them. "It was a long time ago, but it seems like yesterday. We'd all seen the lights, on the system Don had rigged up. They were there, you know what I'm saying? You couldn't argue with that. We all saw them. Then they went away and we sat around the fire for a couple of hours. One by one, the guys started getting sleepy and going off into their tents, till it's just me and Don, Jasmine, Jane, and Danny, and maybe one or two others. And all of a sudden, Jasmine just kind of lies down and she starts shaking, and her breathing is going crazy. And then she starts talking, man, but in a voice that is not like her own. And it says how she and Danny are kind of chosen to spread the word, and Don is like the rock on which they will build their temple or something, and the rest of us were going to create new paths. I don't remember the words exactly." He paused, nodding. "But then she comes out with this. And I felt myself go cold inside, you know what I'm saying to you? It was like cold terror went right through me. She says that Jasmine and Danny have to go down this track, it's like half a mile long, through this forest which is like a jungle, at two o'clock in the morning, to a clearing down there. On their own. And in that clearing they are going to have a close encounter. I'm not kidding. I was shitting myself. I was thinking, please, God, don't let them call me. Please don't let them call me."

Dehan was watching him like a cat watching a mouse. "So what happened?"

"I guess Don was feeling like me, and he says no way, man. Danny can go if he wants to, but there is no way Jasmine is going. He was crazy about her back then. He doted on her every move. You know what I'm saying? She was the love of his life. And he said, no way."

I scratched my chin. "How did she feel about that?"

"To be honest? I think she was kind of relieved. And I think it meant a lot to her that he didn't let her go. But for him . . ." He shook his head. "For him it was a catastrophe. It destroyed him as a man."

Dehan frowned at him. "Yeah? Why?"

I said, "In what way did it destroy him, Mr. Estevez?"

He studied Dehan's face a moment, then he studied mine. "Because he blamed himself for what happened next. He never forgave himself. I liked Don, you know? He was not just a friend, he was my mentor, my guide. He was like the father figure I never had at home." He gestured at the dojo around him. "This? This is all thanks to him. Today I am off the streets, believing in myself, teaching other kids that they have other options than crime, because of Don Kirkpatrick. But, man, over the last twenty years I have seen him slowly go to pieces, one week at a time, one month at a time. And all because he blames himself for what happened to Danny."

Dehan flopped back in her chair with her face screwed up like an incredulous fist. "He believes that Danny was punished by aliens for not going to the glade?"

He smiled at her and there was something almost condescending in his expression. "You can laugh, Detective, but that is what Don believes, and I think he's right. How else can you explain what happened on Sunday night? *Or Saturday?* Who knows when it happened? Who knows what happened Saturday, right?"

I raised a hand. "Slow down. Let me get a handle on this. You are telling me that up until Sunday, June seventh, 1998, Donald Kirkpatrick was a loving, doting husband . . ."

Paul was shaking his head. "Not just that, man. He was a different person. He was positive, outgoing, respectful . . ."

"And all of this changed that weekend."

He nodded. "Not overnight. But in the following weeks. He blamed himself for Danny's death. He tortured himself. We talked about it many times, and he cannot get past the question, 'What if

I had let them go?' What if he had let Jasmine and Danny go to that glade? Would Danny be alive today? And every time, I ask him, but what if they had both been killed? Wouldn't you be even more responsible?" He shrugged, spread his hands, and shook his head. "I think he did the right thing. I think he did what any man would have done. I know for sure I would not have let my wife go to that glade, alone, to encounter a fucking alien spacecraft! No way, man!"

I sat and absently scratched my head for a while. I heard Dehan ask, "Going back to something you said earlier. You said it might have happened on Saturday. But Saturday you were all at a party..."

He made a face. "Not really. We were all pretty freaked out by what happened Friday night, and the party broke up pretty early. Most of us left before Danny, and as far as we were concerned, he went home. So to be honest with you, none of us has any idea where he was from Saturday night until Monday morning. At some point, for some reason, he decided to go to Soundview Park. But having said that, if you have read any accounts of abduction cases, people can be gone for a day or more, and then suddenly turn up some random place. You know what I'm saying to you? So, you know, maybe he was taken on his way home, they did whatever to him, and then put him down in the park, and—*bam* —zapped him. I don't know what to tell you."

I repeated, half to myself, "Nobody knows where he was from Saturday night till Monday morning . . . What time did he leave the party?"

He thought about it for a moment. "You'd have to ask Don. I left maybe four or five in the evening, at the latest."

I turned and stared at Dehan. She stared back at me.

He watched us a moment and said, "You heard about the lights, right? The lights over the park?"

I nodded. "Did you see them?"

"Yeah, I did. I lived on Randall at that time. A friend called me. He knew I was into all that stuff. I went out and I saw it.

Somebody got a film. I know. Did you know that? It was in the papers and on TV. Don contacted them and got a copy. You should talk to him and get him to show you."

"I'll do that."

Outside the office we could hear people arriving and going into the dressing rooms, the soft murmur of voices and occasional laughter. He glanced at the clock and smiled at us apologetically. "I'm not involved in that stuff much anymore. I stay in touch with Don and he, well . . ." He shook his head again. "He can't seem to let it go. I tell him he should realize how lucky he is with his wife. She adores him, if only he could see it, and he doesn't treat her right, the way he should. I tell him, 'Let go of the past, man. See what you have in the present!' But all he can see is that night, and Danny's death. He loved Danny, you know? We all did. You couldn't help but love him."

He shrugged and spread his hands. "I'm sorry, Detectives, that's all I can tell you, and as you can see, my students are here. If there is nothing else . . . ?"

We stood and left him to his class. Outside, the shadows were growing long in the late-afternoon sun. We crossed the road at a slow run, and I unlocked the door to the Jag and stopped, leaning on the roof, staring across at Dehan. I could see myself duplicated in the lenses of her sunglasses, staring back at myself across the vast, warped ocean of burgundy.

I gave a small laugh. "I confess to you, Dehan, right now, I am at a loss to explain this. I can't even begin to put together a theory."

She heaved a very big sigh and pulled open the door. "I know."

She climbed in and I climbed in after her. The doors slammed and I said, "Steak, Dehan. This calls for steak, and wine. Maybe that will restore our perspective."

I fired up the beast and we took off toward the shopping mall.

SEVEN

Maria, the desk sergeant, leered at us across the sergeant's desk.

"Morning, you two. The inspector wants to see you in his office." Dehan made for the stairs without answering. Maria winked at me. "You been on holiday again?"

I smiled with dead eyes. "Special ops in Iraq."

"Bit of bang bang in the sand dunes, huh?"

I ignored her and climbed the stairs in silence. Dehan banged on the inspector's door and entered with a face like a summons.

He was his usual, cordial, urbane self, only more so. "Detectives, good morning. Please, come in and sit down. Coffee?"

Dehan didn't say anything, so I answered for both of us and said, "No, thank you, sir."

We sat. He sat. And we all looked at each other in silence. Finally, he said, "So, what cold case are we on at the moment?"

"Danny Brown, twenty years ago, Soundview Park..."

He nodded like he knew the case, but his narrowed eyes said he didn't.

"The body was incinerated, but the feet and the head were not..."

"Oh, yes, the UFO case. Very challenging. And this is what

has kept you away since Thursday. We are now at . . ." He peered at his calendar like he didn't know what day it was. ". . . Tuesday."

I smiled and scratched my head. "Yes, sir. Well, we had the weekend free, but Friday and Monday we were . . ."

He made a humorous face that was not unkind and suggested, "In the field."

I sighed and nodded. "Yes, sir. In the field."

"Like federal agents."

He seemed to expect a response, but Dehan was closed up like a sulking clam. I said, "An unusual series of coincidences, sir, that conspired . . ." I trailed off. He watched me a moment, still smiling, then turned his bland smile on Dehan.

"You are uncharacteristically quiet this morning, Carmen."

After a moment, she said, "Yes, sir."

He sighed and looked down at his blotter. "I make it a matter of personal policy to stay out of the private lives of my detectives, and officers generally, really. I trust all of you, and you two more than most." He looked up. "As far as I am concerned, you have proved yourselves beyond question, and often gone beyond the call of duty."

Dehan was frowning, like she was expecting a trap.

I said, "Thank you, sir."

He sat back. "I am always here for my officers, but personally, I don't care what goes on in your private lives . . ." He held up one finger. "With one, major caveat: as long as you don't bring it to work with you. As long as it does not interfere with your work, or interfere with the quality of your investigation." He frowned down at his hands and nodded repeatedly, as though they were secretly saying something interesting to him. "I think I have made myself clear and I need say no more."

Dehan swallowed and I took a deep breath. "Perfectly clear, sir."

We stood, and as Dehan stepped out of the office ahead of me, the inspector called me back.

"Oh, John . . ."

FIRE FROM HEAVEN | 47

I stopped and turned. "Yes, sir?"

"We have interrogation rooms, you know." He smiled. "You might try conducting some of your interviews there, occasionally. And, John, I don't quite know how to say this. Let me be blunt. It has come as no surprise to anybody. We've all known for a long time. And we are all very happy for you. There will be some teasing, of course, so try to make sure Carmen weathers it with good humor."

I gave him my best lopsided smile and nodded. "Thank you, sir."

Dehan was waiting for me on the stairs.

"What was that?"

"What was what?"

"Why'd he call you back?"

I turned to face her. I stepped in close, held her shoulders, and smiled at her. "He told me it has come as no surprise to anybody. They all knew long before we did. Everybody is very happy for us and they wish us well. There will be some good-natured razzing, but we should take it in good part. Now, let's get back to work. We have a murder to solve."

She nodded and we went down to the detectives' room. Mo was at his desk leering at us as we approached. Dehan dropped into her chair and he called over, "Hey, where you been all weekend . . . ?"

He was about to go on, but I replied in a loud voice that just about everybody could hear, "I responded to an emergency call."

He raised an eyebrow. "Yeah? Who from . . . ?"

Again I cut him short. "Your wife." I dropped into my chair and smiled at him. A few other detectives were looking over and grinning. "She said she hadn't got laid in ten years and she was about to have an aneurism. Luckily I got to her in time. It took me all weekend to fix the problem, though."

His face turned crimson.

"Any more questions, Mo? No?" I pointed at the work on his desk. "How about trying to make an arrest this semester?"

There was some suppressed chuckling around the room. I turned back to my own desk and picked up the phone. Dehan was typing furiously at her laptop, but I could see her shoulder shaking silently.

The phone rang a couple of times and a pretty voice answered. "Hello?"

"Good morning, is this Jane Harrison?"

"Speaking."

"This is Detective John Stone of the NYPD. We run a cold-case unit and we are looking into the homicide of Danny Brown . . ."

"Danny? My goodness . . . That was twenty years ago, at least!"

"It was almost exactly twenty years ago. I was wondering if you could spare us some time to answer a few questions."

"Of course, but I'm not sure I can tell you anything useful. I imagine you're at the Forty-Third?"

I told her we were, and she said, "Okay, you're in luck. I have the day off. I work in TV production at NBC and my timetable is pretty erratic. I can be there in less than half an hour."

I thanked her and hung up.

Dehan spoke without looking at me. "I've been trying to find the footage of the lights. No luck so far. Most of the local papers carried articles on it, but the most comprehensive one was in the *Fortean Times*." She shook her head. "I can't see that any of them has anything more than we know already."

I flopped back and stared at her. "And we know practically nothing."

She nodded, met my eye, crossed her arms, leaned back, mirroring my movement, and began to speak. "They all drove up to the mountain. They saw lights in the sky on his scanner. Jasmine went into a trance and said she and Danny should go to the glade." She wagged a finger at me. "That's a turning point. Donald says no. They return to Donald's house. We don't know when exactly, but presumably sometime in the morning. But by

FIRE FROM HEAVEN | 49

six in the evening, everybody's had enough, and instead of the party they had planned, they all go home—and this is the second turning point. Because now Danny disappears. How far is it from Don's house to Danny's? Less than a mile. He could walk it in a quarter of an hour or twenty minutes max. But somewhere between Pugsley Avenue and Lacombe, Danny vanishes off the face of the Earth and is gone for somewhere between twenty-four and thirty-six hours."

I studied her in silence for a while, then added, "And during that time he is incinerated and dismembered. We don't know how."

"Incinerated, dismembered, and *placed* carefully, leaving no tracks."

"For no reason."

"What?"

I shook my head, then shrugged and spread my hands. "What's the motive? Nobody made an insurance killing on him, nobody inherited anything of value, nobody got rich from his death. He was single, everybody liked him . . . What was the motive?"

Dehan sighed and rubbed her face. "It's not hard," she said at last. "It's not hard to see how Don Kirkpatrick and Detective Ochoa wound up concluding what they did. The parallel is there. We go over to Africa and we slaughter elephants, buffalo, lions— and we do it without motive. We do it for fun. So what they are proposing is that other beings come to Earth and do the same thing."

I grinned. "You becoming a believer, Scully?"

"Take a hike. I'm saying it's easy to see why somebody would come to that conclusion."

I screwed up my face.

She arched an eyebrow. "What? Now *you* are the skeptic?"

"Thing is, Dehan, even if you do accept the extraterrestrial hypothesis, there are questions that have no satisfactory answer."

"Like?"

"Like why didn't they kill Donald? Why didn't they kill Jasmine? Paul, Jane, Dixon, and all the others? Danny was the only one who was actually keen to go to the glade. But he's the one who gets killed."

She thought about it. "Okay, I'm not saying I buy this, but we're exploring the idea, right?"

"Right."

"So they said that Don was the rock on which they were going to build. So maybe they wanted him for that."

"So are they simply hunters or have they a mission here?" I shook my head. "It lacks consistency. Even if they wanted to preserve Don and Jasmine for some reason, why only kill one of them? And why wait till he's back in the Bronx? Why not kill him out in the mountains? If they are hunters, they could have had a field day out there in the forest."

"Maybe they were not hunters. Maybe they were scientists conducting a sociological experiment that went wrong. Maybe he was taken up, and they were beaming him down to a discreet location near his home, and the transporter went wrong. That would be more consistent."

I smiled at her for a moment. She picked up a pencil, stared at it, and threw it on the desk. "Listen to me. Next thing, I'm going to be wearing a tinfoil hat."

"Eliminate the impossible, Watson, and whatever is left, *however improbable*..."

"Not helpful."

"Perhaps. But let's be careful about what we eliminate as impossible, when it might simply be highly improbable."

"What are you talking about? Are you switching the tables on me?"

The phone buzzed. I picked it up.

"Stone."

"Detective Stone, you have a Jane Harrison here to see you."

"Okay, thanks." I hung up. "That was fast. She's here. You want to take her up? I'll get coffee."

Ten minutes later, I pushed through the door holding three paper cups of coffee-like substance precariously in my hands. Jane Harrison was in her early forties but looked younger. She was well-dressed in an expensive mulberry suit and had an expensive haircut to go with it.

I set down the coffee and smiled at her as I sat. "It's coffee, Jane, but not as we know it."

She laughed.

I went on, "Thanks for coming in. The case is twenty years cold, and we can use any help we can get."

She gave a small frown. "To be honest, I was pretty surprised to get your call. I thought Donald Kirkpatrick's 'explanation'"— she put inverted commas around the word with her tone of voice —"had been accepted by default."

Dehan frowned. "You don't buy Donald's explanation?"

Jane sighed and thought for a moment before answering. Then she seemed to lock onto Dehan's eyes. "You know the poster? It has a picture of a flying saucer over a woodland, and it says, 'I want to believe.' That was me. That was all of us back then. And it is a really *bad* motto. I want to believe. What does that mean? It means you are going to *interpret* the evidence, it means that when the evidence gives you the wrong answer, you will massage it and even distort it until it gives you the answer you want. And frankly, with hindsight, I think that is what Donald has done. Okay, Danny's death is very hard to explain in conventional terms." She gave a small laugh. "*I* can't explain it! But the fact is there is as little evidence to show he was killed by an alien hunter as there is to show he was killed by a terrestrial drug dealer, loan shark, or jilted lover. When you approach a mystery with that 'I want to believe' attitude, you're screwed before you even begin."

Dehan blinked at her a few times and smiled. "Have you any theories of your own as to what happened?"

She shook her head. "But I can tell you that what happened that weekend was not quite how it is portrayed in Donald's book, or how he describes it at his conferences. There was more to it than that."

I nodded a few times. "Why don't you give us a fuller picture, starting from Friday evening?"

She spread out her hands on the tabletop and stared at her fingers for a long moment. "Probably the first thing I should tell you," she said, "is that Paul and I were engaged to be married."

EIGHT

"Danny and Paul were childhood friends. They used to say they were brothers, but guys say that kind of thing, don't they?" She glanced at me for confirmation.

I offered her an inexpressive smile.

"Whatever. They were real close and obviously loved each other . . ." She glanced at me, startled momentarily by the possibility that I might have misunderstood her. "Not in a weird way. They weren't gay." She laughed. "Just like . . . *guys*. And they were both really into that UFO stuff. Especially Danny. He was crazy about it, and he kind of infected Paul. Paul was interested, but he was also interested in other stuff, like . . ." She hesitated and glanced at Dehan for understanding. "Like *life* . . . right?"

Dehan smiled. "Right."

It was a neutral statement, but Jane took it as encouragement and laughed. "Like movies, dancing, a restaurant now and then. And hey! We can talk about books that *aren't* about the alien presence on Earth!"

I gave her an "I know exactly what you mean" chuckle and said, "But hang on a moment, are we talking about Paul or Danny here?"

She stared at me for five whole seconds, which when you are

staring at somebody is a long time. "You don't miss much, do you?"

"No."

She sighed. "It was kind of odd, because it was like Danny was obsessed with UFOs and *The X-Files* and that whole world, but somehow he made it fascinating. Plus he was funny, happy, *inexhaustible*, and he just made you feel alive by simply being in his presence. But Paul . . ." She flopped back in her chair and sighed again. It was a sigh of real regret. "Paul was obsessed with Danny! I guess we all were to a greater or lesser extent. Or, if not obsessed, at least kind of really *aware* of him, *all the time* . . . you know?"

I nodded. "I feel you are leading up to something, Jane . . ."

"Yeah, I am. I'm sorry. I'm getting there, but it takes some explaining. So, Danny's whole life was his UFO research. Which was, in a sense, why I was with Paul. With Paul, we could go out to the cinema, or watch a movie at home, maybe sometimes go out to dinner or whatever. We had a life that included more things than just aliens. But, sooner or later, the conversation would *always* come back to Danny."

She paused, staring down at her hands. After a moment, she looked up and searched Dehan's face. I thought I saw a hint of guilt, a plea for understanding. She went on.

"With Danny, the subject always came back to UFOs. With Paul, the subject always came back to Danny. I fought it, I really did, but bit by bit I began to lose respect for him."

Dehan nodded a few times, and in a voice that was not unsympathetic she said, "It sounds to me, Jane, as though all along the one you were in love with was Danny."

"That obvious, huh?"

"You said so yourself at the beginning. The only reason you were not with Danny was because his whole life was UFOs."

"I said that? Yeah, I guess I said that."

I sat back. "So what happened?"

"Something you have to understand is that Danny never fell in love. There just wasn't a woman on Earth who could keep up with him, and he needed a woman who would not just keep up, but would challenge him. So he never gave his heart to anyone. But he was the ultimate flirt. He didn't even know he was flirting. He didn't care if she was ninety, two, a drop-dead gorgeous supermodel, a homeless tramp, or the First Lady. It was all the same to him. If she was female, he would flirt with her. Just because flirting was fun. He would make her laugh, tease her, make her feel good about herself. And believe me, if you were a woman and you spoke to Danny for two minutes, you felt like a million bucks." She smiled. It was a private smile between her and some special memory. "I guess there were not many girls who didn't have a bit of a crush on him."

I scratched my chin. "Jane, did Danny have occasional girlfriends? Did he have passing affairs...?"

"Yeah. They weren't quite one-night stands, but you knew that if you hit the sack with Danny, it would not develop into anything serious." She laughed again, without much humor. "They were more like three- or four-night stands. He never lied or pretended. I guess he slept with most of the girls in the group, and some who were not in the group. He was hard to resist."

"Where did these encounters take place?"

Her cheeks colored a little. "His parents were pretty liberal, and if he took a girl home to meet them it was generally accepted that she would stay the night. But they drew the line if the girl had a boyfriend, or if they *knew* she had a boyfriend. So he had a van."

Dehan raised an eyebrow. "A van?"

"Yeah. Sometimes we would use it to go on field trips. It was pretty luxurious in the back. He had music." She smiled and shook her head. "He told us what it was for."

We fell silent for a moment, and I drummed my fingers on the table. "Okay, Jane, we have been talking around this for a while. Do you think it's time to get to the point?"

She nodded a few times, then took a deep, reluctant breath.

"Paul and I didn't have a row or anything. We didn't start arguing or anything like that. I truly believe he was not aware that there was a problem. But I had grown really *bored* with him. With him and his kind of adulation of the ground Danny walked on. And at the same time, my attraction for Danny was growing to the point where I was kidding myself that maybe I could be the one. Stupid, I know, but that was how it was.

"On the Friday night, we all went up to Macomb Mountain. Donald had his equipment there and we were trying to pick up signals or transmissions that might confirm there was a non-terrestrial presence in the atmosphere, the stratosphere, or even just in orbit. He also had some kind of visual scanner that could pick up light beyond either end of the visible spectrum. I'm no scientist, but the equipment seemed pretty sophisticated to me.

"So, around midnight we picked up some signals that Don said were not naturally occurring, and were not of human origin. I don't know how he knew that, but he did. And then we saw lights in the sky..."

I asked, "Visible to the naked eye?"

"Uh-uh, no, on the scanner. And they were moving at incredible speeds. Accelerating naught to a thousand miles an hour instantly, then stopping dead, reversing, turning right angles. Crazy stuff you normally only read about in books. It was pretty exciting and we were all pretty high."

"High?"

"No! No, not high. None of us was into that. No, high on adrenaline; on the buzz. So then the lights just vanished. We sat around waiting for them to come back, but they didn't, and finally a bunch of the guys got tired and went into their tents." She paused. "I'm trying to remember who stayed... Danny, obviously, me, Don and Jasmine, and Paul... There may have been some others. The conversation was all between Don and Danny. To say they were excited would be a huge understatement. They were tripping. Then, it must have been about two in the morning, Jasmine suddenly freaks out and starts having this kind of fit. She's shaking all over and kind of moving her hands and feet. I remember asking Don if she was epileptic. He said she wasn't, but he was looking for something to put between her teeth to stop her from biting her tongue. We were all sort of, what the hell do we do?" She stopped, shrugged, and blinked a few times. "Then it just stopped. She lay still, on her back, with her eyes closed, and started talking."

I leaned forward. "Have you read Don's book?"

She shook her head. "No. I didn't want to."

"Have you discussed what happened that night with many people?"

"I lost touch with the group immediately after what happened, and I think this is probably one of the only times I have discussed it with anybody in all this time. Why?"

I nodded. "Okay, good, I would like you to try and be as accurate and precise as possible about what happened next, and in particular about what Jasmine said."

She looked a little surprised. "Okay." She thought for a moment. "It was like it wasn't really her talking. Her voice kind of changed. It was deeper, kind of weird. And she said . . . I can't remember it verbatim, Detective Stone, but basically she said that each of us there had some kind of function, or purpose, but that she and Danny were like their messengers or spokespeople, and that they should go up a path—it was a path we had explored earlier that led to a kind of clearing—and there they would have a close encounter with these beings."

She closed her eyes and shook her head. "I am not proud of my feelings right then. You know, maybe I am just really shallow. Everybody else there was, like, blown away because we were making contact with ET, and these two guys were going to carry their message to mankind. But me, all I could think of was why was it Jasmine going up that path with Danny and not me?

"So when Don turns around and says, no way, he will not allow Jasmine to go, I was the happiest chick in the world. So he is saying 'Either we all go, or nobody goes!,' most of the others are saying we should follow the aliens' instructions to the letter, and me, I am saying, let me and Danny go. You know, like a compromise. And then Don got real mad, and he started quoting cases at us about where humans had been abducted and mutilated. Um . . . he quoted Darlington, Ohio, in 1958, Sergeant Lovette in New Mexico in 1956, Guarapiranga in Brazil, in the 1980s, 1988, I think. And several other cases . . ."

She trailed off. We waited a bit, but she just sat and bit her lips. Finally, I said, "What about these cases, Jane?"

"Well, you've heard of cattle mutilation?"

"Something. Not much."

"Well, Detective, however skeptical you are, this is something that has been going on in the Midwest for at least forty years and even the FBI don't know what to make of it. It's a problem, because ranchers are losing stock, sometimes by the hundreds, and in every case the genitals, the lips, and other parts of the anatomy have been surgically removed, without leaving any trace of blood, or any tracks. There is basically no sign that there was anybody there. You go and talk to those ranchers, and we have, and they'll all tell you they have seen lights in the sky at night, and in the morning they go and they have five, six, seven—sometimes more—dead cows, all surgically mutilated. Now, each one of those animals weighs half a ton. And there isn't a trace of blood, a tire track, a footprint . . ."

She paused. "Now, what Don was telling us that night was that this also happened to people, but it's something that is hushed up even within the UFO community, and he listed a number of cases where people had been found exsanguinated, surgically mutilated, with genitals and other parts of their body removed; and in some cases with parts of their body incinerated. As with the cattle, no trace of any person or vehicle was ever found near the body. In the light of those cases, he insisted that if anybody went, we should all go together." She stopped and studied the expression on my face for a moment, then smiled unhappily. "If you have contacts in the FBI, check with them. You know they visited most of us after Danny's death? This is real, Detective."

FIRE FROM HEAVEN | 59

"It's also a hell of a coincidence."

"Maybe. But I can tell you that I had nightmares for two years, thinking about what might have happened to us if I had persuaded Danny that we should go to that glade, that he should go with me instead of Jasmine. I had to see a therapist in the end."

I grunted. "So in the morning you went back to Donald's house?"

She nodded. "Yeah. We were supposed to have a barbeque, a party, and chill. Don was cool like that. He and Jasmine were older than the rest of us, but they were fun."

Dehan frowned. "Don? Don was fun?"

"Sure. Have you met him yet? He's cool. I miss him sometimes. Real smart, intelligent, a real open mind. And lots of fun." She laughed. "And when he and Danny started hitting off each other, they'd crack you up. They were good times. But that night we were all just kind of freaked out."

"So you went home early."

She didn't answer straightaway. She stared down at her hands on the table for a while, then heaved a big sigh and said, "Not exactly. I am really not proud of what I did that day. I behaved like a total bitch. I kind of lost it, and all Saturday I just came on to Danny big-time. It freaked him out, it upset everybody, and it really upset Paul. At first Danny took it as a joke, but as I kept on pushing, he started to back off. Paul started getting mad. Like, he went really cold and wouldn't talk to Danny." She hesitated a moment. "In retrospect, I guess that was what I wanted, to break them up. So I pushed harder. When Danny wouldn't respond, I got mad too, and around four, everybody started to leave. It was a pretty crazy weekend. Paul took me home and we broke up in the car."

I said, "Was it mutual?"

She made a face. "Kind of. I wanted it, I was tired of him, but he broke up with me. He told me he never wanted to see me again. What made him really mad was not that I had betrayed him, but that I had broken his friendship with Danny."

Dehan asked, "He phrased it like that, with those words?"

"Pretty much, yeah."

The room fell silent for a long moment. Finally, I sighed and said, "You have given us a lot to think about, Jane. Thank you for being so candid. I just have one more question. Paul is a martial arts instructor. Was he already into the martial arts when you were engaged to him?"

"Oh yeah, all his life, since he was like six years old."

"Tae kwon do?"

"Not just tae kwon do, though that was his main discipline, also kendo and ninjitsu."

I stared at her, wondering if she realized what she had just told me. I was pretty sure she didn't. Dehan saw her to the door while I sat and stared at the table and thought about Danny and Paul—and the FBI.

NINE

Dehan returned to her desk, and I stepped out to stroll under the plane trees on Story Avenue while I phoned Bernie at the bureau. It was warm, not yet the oppressive heat of July, but moving that way, and the dappled shade of the trees was welcome.

"Yeah, Stone, what's up, my friend?"

"Bernie, listen, I have a very unusual request."

"All of your requests are unusual, Stone. It's what makes you so loveable—that and your hot partner. What makes this one different?"

"Yeah, I know, but this one is special. Listen, twenty years ago, June eighth, 1998, there was a murder in Soundview Park. It was never solved..."

"Yeah, I know, you're doing the cold cases. Okay, how can I help?"

"This case has some very unusual features, Bernie, and it seems your boys at the bureau may have got involved."

"In a homicide? That's local PD's brief. What was in it for the bureau?"

I stopped in the shade of a tree and stared down at the sidewalk, thinking about what I was about to say. Finally, I said it. "Bernie, the victim was one Danny Brown, a UFO researcher, and there's circumstantial evidence that he might have been killed by a UFO..."

I could hear the smile in his voice. "You're kidding, right?"

"No, I'm not kidding, Bernie. And please note, I am not saying that I *believe* he was, only that there is circumstantial evidence. And also note, Bernie, that the *U* in UFO stands for 'unidentified.'"

He snorted. "Okay."

"However, the detective who had the case back then now believes the victim was in fact killed by an ET, and, the night he was killed, several hundred people saw an unidentified flying object over Soundview Park at the spot where he was killed. So, I am not saying this lightly."

"Okay, Stone. I hear you. What do you want?"

"I want you to listen to me. The UFO was seen by hundreds of witnesses, it was reported in the press—whatever it was, Bernie, it was *there*. That is not a matter of opinion. It's a fact. So, here is where you can help me. Several of the people who were involved with the victim in his research claim that they were visited by agents who purported to be Feds. They say they were told by these agents to keep quiet about the murder, and about what had happened."

"Holy shit."

"My feelings precisely. As of right now, I am more interested in the bureau's involvement than in the ETs. So, I would like to interview those agents, and I need you to find out, A, if it is true that they went to see the witnesses and, B, if so, will they talk to me about it? And Bernie, make them understand I am not using official channels as a courtesy..."

"Yeah, okay. But you do realize, Stone, that the FBI does not have a department specializing in supernatural phenomena or UFOs. That's just fiction."

"I know that, Bernie. I also know that the bureau has investigated both from time to time, when it has considered there might be a threat to national security."

"Okay, I'll make some inquiries and get back to you."

"I appreciate it. Oh, and Bernie..."

"Yuh?"

"What do you know about cattle mutilation?"

"Ah, jeez! Do you know how many people ask me about that? That was, like, forty years ago out in the Midwest. Some ranchers complained that their cattle were being slaughtered and mutilated. We were asked to investigate, but the bureau had no jurisdiction in a case like that. How is that a federal matter, right? I think we investigated a case on an Indian reservation because we had jurisdiction there and there was political pressure to do something. It turned out to be coyotes or some such. But the conspiracy theory websites get hold of this stuff, you know? And they make something out of nothing."

I nodded, even though he couldn't see me. "Okay, Bernie, thanks, I appreciate it. We need to get together sometime. You owe me I don't know how many drinks."

"Yeah, right. Stop talking about it and do it already!"

We laughed. He told me he'd get back to me and hung up.

I strolled back toward the station house deep in thought, came to my car, and paused to rest my ass on the hood. After staring at nothing for a while, I called Donald Kirkpatrick. It rang twice and his voice, severe and impatient, said, "Yes!"

"Mr. Kirkpatrick, this is Detective Stone. Good morning."

He seemed to soften a bit. "Oh, Detective. What can I do for you?"

"I keep hearing about somebody who got footage of the lights over Soundview Park that night. Have you ever seen that film?"

"Yes. I own the original. I bought it from the person who made it, when I decided to write my book."

"May I see it?"

He seemed to hesitate for a moment. "Yes, of course. Are you coming to the talk tomorrow?"

"Wouldn't miss it for the world."

"Good. Then after the conference, we can have a look at it."

"Great. Mr. Kirkpatrick, before I let you go. You never mentioned that Paul Estevez and Jane Harrison were engaged."

"Should I have?"

"Well, in view of the fact that they broke off their engagement on the night Danny was murdered, do you not think that was relevant?"

"Not really. Why should it be?"

"Do you know why they broke up?"

"No. It's none of my business, Detective."

"Apparently they had a row at your house."

"I was not aware of it. They were terribly young at the time, Detective Stone. People of that age are always getting emotional about their relationships. Frankly, after the experiences we had just had on Macomb Mountain, I couldn't have been less interested in Jane and Paul's relationship."

"How about Danny? Was he involved with anybody?"

"Not that I am aware of." He gave a snort that might have been a laugh. "Danny was a remarkable young man, and eminently sensible. Too sensible to tie himself to any kind of long-term relationship."

"Yeah," I said. "Yeah, that is the impression I am beginning to get. Thank you, Mr. Kirkpatrick. I'll see you tomorrow evening."

I hung up and watched Dehan step out of the station house and stand for a moment, looking around. She spotted me and crossed the road at a slow run.

"You hiding, Mr. Stone?" She didn't wait for an answer. "I've been looking for the movie of the lights. I don't think it was ever uploaded to YouTube. I contacted NBC, who ran it on the news at..."

She stopped because I was shaking my head. "Kirkpatrick has it. He's going to bring it along tomorrow night for us to see."

She narrowed her eyes and nodded, then pointed at me. "You the man."

"I also asked Bernie to put us in touch with the agents who—allegedly—spoke to the witnesses. We'll see where that leads. Maybe we'll both get abducted, or visited by men in black."

She sat next to me and chewed her lip, staring at the blacktop. "So now we have a motive. Jealousy."

"Mm-hm..."

"And he's Latino. Latinos can be *very* jealous."

"Is that so?"

She nodded. "Yup." Then she shrugged and peered at me in the sunshine. "It doesn't help us much, because, with a guy like Danny, we might have a hundred motives. There is no telling how many girls he was sleeping with."

I studied her face a moment and was struck for the thousandth time by how exquisite it was. "Yeah, it could be a jealous husband, a jealous boyfriend, a woman scorned..." I shook my head and shrugged my shoulders. "Or any variation on that theme. But, what does help us to narrow it down a bit, or *should* help us, is the way in which the murder was executed. If anything should point out an individual, it is the unique character of this murder."

We were both silent for a moment. Because, despite my insightful observation, unless it was a jealous alien or a jilted alien, the nature of the murder did not immediately point to anybody.

Then Dehan said, "One thing that did strike me was that Paul practices kendo. Samurai swords, if they are well made, can be as sharp as razor blades. And a real expert can split a lentil in half with a single strike. Paul is a seventh dan in tae kwon do, Stone, I saw the marks on his belt. Believe me, that guy can kill you fifteen different ways in fifteen seconds, and he has control and precision in his strikes."

I studied her a moment. "So we are saying, what? That he beheaded Danny at some other location..."

"Hence the absence of blood."

"Then cut off his feet and his genitals and, somehow, in a way we do not yet understand, placed the body in the park..."

"... Set up the hoax with the UFO and the lasers, and got away, in a way we do not yet understand, without leaving any prints." She sighed. "It is the seedling of a theory."

I shook my head. "The only part of this theory that makes any sense to me at the moment is the castration. If we are dealing with jealousy or a scorned lover, castration makes sense. But decapitation, cutting off the feet, UFOs . . ." I sighed. "But I'll tell you what my main problem with it is. This homicide went down one of two ways: either it is genuinely what it appears to be, and we simply don't understand the motivation and thinking of the killer because he, she, it, or they are literally alien; or it was very carefully planned and executed. Now, if what Jane has told us is accurate, Paul simply did not have the time to plan and execute the murder. So the only person we know of with a motive did not have the means."

She grunted. Overhead, a pigeon landed clumsily in the tree, beating its wings noisily against the canopy. A couple of uniforms stood in the sunshine across the road, talking and laughing. One went inside, the other walked toward a car, fitting on his hat with both hands. It was all very normal, very mundane.

"Unless," Dehan said abruptly, "Jane was as oblivious to Paul's thoughts and feelings as she thought he was to hers."

I frowned. "Talk me through."

"Think about it. He is fixated on her and Danny. He doesn't want to lose either of them. So he is *paying attention* to both of them. He is very aware of both of them. But Jane is fixated on Danny, not Paul. So she is super aware of everything Danny says, everything he does. She is paying attention. However, she is *not* paying attention to what Paul is saying or doing—or *feeling*! She told us. She said he was boring her. All she could think about is Danny . . ."

"Okay, I get it, but what's your point?"

"My point is, she told us that Paul didn't notice that she was falling for Danny, but she was wrong. What happened was that *she didn't notice that he had noticed.* Because she wasn't paying attention to him. But Paul did notice, and at some point he began to get jealous. He began to get mad. And then—" She jabbed a finger on my shoulder. "He started to plan. He started to plan how he was going to eliminate Danny from the picture and get his revenge."

I looked at her for a moment, then pointed at her the way she had pointed at me. "*That*, Detective Dehan, is the seedling of a theory. *That* begins to ring true. Now we just have to answer the question, how does a two-hundred-and-twenty-pound man arrange to carry the remains of his friend into the park without leaving prints, and . . . and . . ." I wagged a finger at her. ". . . remember, the rain was not something he would necessarily have predicted. Not in June. In fact, all of the events that apparently led up to the murder were not predictable."

She stood, pursed her lips, and shoved her hands in her back pockets. Then she walked in a slow semicircle around me and back again, stopped, and shook her head. "No. You are still thinking along the lines that the events of that night were the *motive* for the killing. But like you said in the beginning, let's home in closer and dissect this a little more. Think of it this way, that the events of that night were just *symptomatic* of the motive to kill. Like I said before, this was something that had been building up for some time. He's been aware, maybe since the beginning, that the man Jane really wants is Danny. His jealousy and his hatred have been building over time. The plan was already laid—all but ready.

"Now, if that is true, Stone, that takes us back into March, maybe even earlier. And if *that* is true, the planning would have *had* to take into account the likelihood of rain, and include some way of crossing muddy terrain without leaving prints. Jane's attack of jealousy against Jasmine and her flirtation with Danny may have been the trigger, but the round was already loaded and the hammer was cocked."

"A nicely rounded metaphor, Dehan."

"Thank you. And Jasmine's trance was probably something

that was going to happen sooner or later anyway. As it was, when it happened, it set off the whole series of events that followed, and drove Paul to execute the plan he had been developing for several months."

I thought about it. "It's good. It's coherent. It's motive." I looked at her. "But the question remains, how did he do it? And it raises another question too. Where?"

She became suddenly very serious, stepped close to me, and placed her hand on my chest.

"Where? Right there in the park. What if . . ." She paused. "What if Paul gets home, his rage is out of control. He's had enough. He calls Danny and says he wants to meet him. They both live nearby. Paul suggests the park. It isn't raining yet. Paul brings along his sword. He decapitates Danny. Death would be instant. He would not bleed a lot. He cuts off the feet and the genitals, not just relieving his rage but making it look like one of the mutilations Don has just told them about. Then he drags the body over to the location, sets it up, and leaves . . ."

"What about . . . ?"

"Wait! He goes to his car, which he has parked nearby, and he brings with him his remote-controlled UFO—part of the plan he had already developed. He douses the body in petrol, then sets off the UFO to attract viewers and press. The UFO starts flashing its lights. Now, here's the clever part. He has rigged a small, battery-powered ignition device and linked it to the remote control, to spark when the UFO starts firing its lasers, and ignite the petrol. The body is burned and, later, it starts to rain, and the small amount of blood left where the body was killed is washed away into the soil. In the morning we are left with the mystery of an alien murder. After that, leave it to Don's conscience to build up the mythology surrounding the case. What am I?"

"That is very clever. You are very clever."

"Tell me again, but use another word, not clever. What am I?"

"Smart. You are very . . ."

FIRE FROM HEAVEN

"*Brilliant!* I am *brilliant*! Me Holmes, you Watson. Suck it up, Stone, man. Ha!"

I raised an eyebrow at her. "It is a very compelling theory, my dear Dehan. How do we prove it?"

She thought for a moment, looking up at the leaves on the London plane trees.

"After twenty years, physical and forensic evidence is out of the question. So we haul Paul in, present him with what Jane has told us, and scare him into confessing."

TEN

But Paul was out of town till the next day.

I called Frank at the ME's and asked him to dig out the ME's report on the case, which he did and emailed it over. I printed two copies and gave one to Dehan. We read it in detail and found it contained nothing we didn't already know. That night, and much of the next day, we spent reading Donald Kirkpatrick's book, *Heaven's Fire*. It was well written and extremely persuasive.

It was structured in two parts. The first part of the book dealt with the question of UFOs generally and made a strong case that there was an extraterrestrial presence on Earth. It argued that since the end of World War II, Western governments had been engaged in a cover-up, concealing the truth about the presence of ET on Earth. The reason for the cover-up was not clear, and he admitted that all he had was speculation. But much of his speculation was based on strong evidence that made some kind of sense: avoiding mass panic, using technology recovered from Roswell against the Soviet Union during the Cold War, and a more far-fetched theory involving a secret war with the aliens.

He didn't prove his case, he left many questions unanswered, but he made a well-reasoned, compelling argument with lots of circumstantial evidence.

The second part of the book dealt with Danny's murder. It set out to prove, in his own words, that Danny had been "deliberately killed by an alien, extraterrestrial presence." He did not start, as I had expected him to, with the events of the two days leading up to Danny's death. Instead, he went into a detailed analysis of the many cases of cattle mutilation in the Midwest since the 1970s. It did not agree, in any way, with what Bernie had told me.

According to Kirkpatrick, Senator Floyd K. Haskell had asked the FBI for help, back in 1975, because of growing public concern about well over a hundred mutilations that had taken place in Colorado alone. But by 1979, the FBI had reported that there had been an estimated eight thousand mutilations in Colorado, causing somewhere in the region of one million dollars' worth of damage.

The mutilations were all very similar. The incisions were always surgical in nature, clean and precise. In most cases the animals were drained of blood, but there was never any sign of blood in the immediate area of the slaughter.

One of the features that Kirkpatrick pointed to as evidence of ET was the speed with which some of the mutilations were carried out. To illustrate this, he related a case reported by the NIDS of two ranchers in Utah, in 1997, who were tagging their cattle. Having tagged a particular animal, they continued working, just three hundred yards away. Forty-five minutes later, they found the calf completely eviscerated, with all its internal organs missing: no blood, no entrails, no tracks, and as in all the other cases, there were no tracks or footprints around the site of the mutilated animal. It was as though the attackers had approached from the air.

He detailed many similar cases. In the end, the FBI had concluded their investigation and admitted they could not explain how the animals were killed, or why they were killed in that particular way. Local law enforcement continued to investigate, but with no results.

He then went on to list a number of human deaths and mutilations which were very similar in character to the cattle mutilations. These included an unidentified Brazilian man in Guarapiranga who had had all his internal organs removed, along with his lips, eyes, ears, and tongue. He had not bled, and his body had shown no signs of decay after seventy-two hours of his death. The coroner's report was included in the book, with its official seal.

Other cases were listed, like the case of USAF Sergeant Jonathan Lovette and Major Bill Cunningham, in which the major allegedly witnessed the sergeant being abducted by a UFO in the desert near the Holloman Air Base. His body turned up three days later, expertly exsanguinated and eviscerated. Just like the cows in the Midwest. Just like the man at Guarapiranga.

By six in the evening, I had not yet come to Danny's death, or the events of that weekend. I dropped the book on the desk and looked at Dehan. She was engrossed in her copy, frowning hard. Without looking at me, she said, "What?"

"Time to go."

She glanced at the clock on the wall. "Let me finish this page."

I stood and put my jacket on. "Come on, Carmencita, I'll take you to see the real thing."

She sighed, put a marker in the page, and stood.

Outside it was still light, but there was a copper quality to the air, the shadows were long, and the birds sounded sleepy. As we climbed into the Jag, she said, "Is this for real, Stone? He is making a damn good case. I can see why a lot of people believe him. I don't mind telling you it is scaring me."

I fired up the engine and pulled out of the lot. As we headed toward Bruckner Boulevard, I made a face and shook my head. "He makes a compelling case for the existence of UFOs. I've got to the cattle mutilations..."

"Same."

"So far, he hasn't proved anything, but he is putting up a

damn good argument. As far as explaining Danny's death . . ." I shrugged. "I haven't got there yet, but I am not seeing it." I glanced at her and smiled. "Besides, what happened to Holmes? I thought you had the whole thing figured out."

She scowled. "You're a son of a bitch, Stone. You knew perfectly well there was no petrol, no accelerant of any sort found in the ashes or the soil. That's why you asked Frank to send over the ME's report."

I nodded. "Yeah, that was a small problem, plus it had been raining on and off all afternoon—Ochoa told us that—so the clay would have been wet long before they got there. And there was another problem . . ."

She looked at me. "You could have told me all this when I came up with the theory."

"But you looked so happy. And, also, there might still be something in it."

"What's the other thing?"

"To incinerate his body to the state it was in, it would have needed around one thousand eight hundred degrees Fahrenheit, sustained for about two hours. Even then, there would have been more bones in the ashes. The boiling point of hydroxyapatite is around one thousand five hundred centigrade, which is about two thousand five hundred degrees Fahrenheit. Hydroxyapatite is a naturally occurring mineral form of calcium, which you would need to evaporate to make bone disintegrate. So either he was burned for over two hours at nearly two thousand degrees, or he was blasted with heat at nearly three thousand degrees for a short while."

She looked out the window at the passing houses as the streetlamps started to come on. "You just happen to know this, about what temperatures bodies burn, and hydroxipa-whatever."

"No, but I have a book on the subject. It's on the shelf at home. I looked it up. Books are good like that."

"Point taken. So we are back to square one."

I shook my head. A car passed with its headlamps on. I leaned forward and switched mine on too. Imperceptibly, dusk moved in and turned the air grainy.

"What you did was show that with a little ingenuity, you *can* make a murder look like the work of aliens."

We drove in silence for a while, but as we turned onto Morris Park Avenue, she suddenly shook her head. "I don't know, Stone. I don't think I did, because, A, the timing of the rain was crucial and, B, even if you remove the rain from the equation, the fact remains, you need about three thousand degrees to burn the body. The cuts on his feet and neck were singed, but the head and feet themselves, his hair and his flip-flops were untouched, just like the grass underneath him. However ingenious his killer was, that is one tall order."

I nodded. I had to admit she was right. And after a moment, she added, "And let's face it, do you see Paul as the type to dream up something that elaborate?"

I shrugged and made a face. "People can surprise you. Sometimes if you overthink something it becomes more complicated than it need be. An uncomplicated mind sees things more clearly."

She grunted. "What do you think?"

I shook my head again. "At the moment I'm trying not to think."

"The way of the empty mind, Sensei? Idiot Do?"

"Something like that."

We left the car in the large parking lot and entered the lobby of the hotel as dusk was shifting to evening. The conference was signposted and we made our way to a large, windowless *L*-shaped room down a blue, carpeted passage. Rows of chairs had been set out facing a table holding a small projector, with a screen set up behind it. The event was well attended. I figured there were maybe seventy or eighty people there, and more were arriving. Among the throng, talking to a man by the projector, I saw the long, lanky figure of Donald Kirkpatrick.

In the foot part of the *L*, opposite the entrance, I saw Jasmine at another table, setting out cups, plastic bottles of water, and jugs of orange juice. I approached her and smiled. She didn't look at me.

I said, "Hello, Jasmine. Do you know if Paul Estevez is here?"

For a moment, she ignored me completely and I thought maybe she hadn't heard me. Then she gave her head a tiny shake and said, "Not yet," turned, and hurried away.

We made our way to the conference section and found a couple of seats at the back, in the corner, where we could observe without being observed. But as it turned out, that was something of a vain hope.

Five minutes later, all the seats were filled, and Kirkpatrick was having a few last words with a man in a blue blazer. I guessed he was the speaker. He was a strongly built, earnest-looking man in his midsixties, with a graying beard and very short, gray hair. The man stepped back, beside the projector, and Kirkpatrick stepped forward, looked out at his audience, and the murmur of conversation hushed. He smiled and instantly looked like a different man. For a moment, I could almost see the man Jane had described to us.

"Welcome," he said, "I am delighted to see so many familiar faces, and a few new ones. Today is a very special day for me. It is twenty years this week that I decided to start researching *Heaven's Fire*, just a couple of weeks after Danny Brown's death. So, in what some might think a futile gesture, I am dedicating this conference, tonight, to the memory of a very remarkable young man. His parents, Stuart and May, are with us tonight, and we extend an especially warm welcome to them."

I had seen them come in a couple of minutes earlier, and now several heads turned to look, there was some friendly waving, and silent mouthing of greetings. Kirkpatrick started talking again.

"We extend also a very warm welcome to Detectives John Stone and Carmen Dehan, who are with us tonight . . ." There was more head turning and staring, but more in astonishment this time than in friendliness. "They are, curiously enough, here tonight because the New York Police Department has decided to reopen the case on Danny's homicide, and we are keen to cooperate as fully as possible. Who knows, they may end up with some very unsuspected suspects."

He smiled, and there was scattered laughter. He became serious again and waited for the laughter to subside.

"I doubt there is a person in this room who is not familiar with the name Danny Brown. To Stuart and May, he was their cherished son. To me, he was like the son I never had. To many, he was an inspiration, for his dedication and energy; to all of us, he was a well-loved friend. It is impossible to conceive that he was anything but that, to anybody. Which is why it is such a tragedy, and such a mystery, that he is not with us tonight. We continue with our mission, in his memory." There was a lot of warm applause. He gestured to the man behind him and said, "Please welcome as our first speaker tonight, a man who needs no introduction, United States of America Air Force Colonel Chad Hait!"

I looked at Dehan. Her eyebrows had shot up all the way to her hairline. Colonel Hait spoke in a voice that was accustomed to being listened to.

"I never had the honor of meeting Danny Brown, but I know how much he meant to most everybody here, and as I address you tonight, I do so with the belief that his death will not be a vain one. I have been researching the subject of UFOs for about forty years, since I was a young pilot stationed across the Atlantic. I have been an active, dedicated investigator for the last twenty of those years. And I can tell you that within the field of UFO research there is one subject that is taboo, one subject that nine out of every ten ufologists will not address—will not even talk about—and that is the possibility that the Visitors are not, as many believe, highly advanced, benign friends and guardians, but hostile predators, just as Professor Stephen Hawking predicted they would be . . ." He paused and looked around the room. "Well, let me tell you." He smiled and gave a small laugh. "And I hope our friends from the NYPD are awake and paying attention, because I have with me here tonight hard, photographic evidence, and sworn testimony, from witnesses in the USA, in Latin America, and in Europe, that *proves beyond any reasonable doubt* that the alien visitors to this planet are hostile. Let me put it simply, ladies and gentlemen: they are here to kill us."

ELEVEN

THE COLONEL CONTINUED IN THAT VEIN FOR THE NEXT sixty minutes. And he was as good as his word. He adduced photographic evidence, and sworn statements, to back up three cases of people who had been killed in inexplicable circumstances, that were all recognizable as what he called 'classic mutilations': they had all had their blood drained out of their bodies, all had at least some organs surgically removed, and in all cases, there were no tracks or footprints in the vicinity.

When he'd finished showing us the last of his slides, he was quiet for a moment, sucking on his teeth. "I'm going to go off on a tangent here for a moment," he said suddenly. "As I have already said, I am glad we have two police officers here tonight, because I want to ask them both a question. I know it's hypothetical, and I know it calls for speculation, but we're among friends here, and nobody is going to hold you to your word, or quote you." There was some scattered laughter. "Detective Dehan, Detective Stone, many of us in this room have had visits from that other law enforcement agency, the Federal Bureau of Investigation, at some time in our lives. Usually they have not been asking for information so much as requiring *us* not to divulge any to anybody else. But on this occasion, as we have you here, let me ask you this: let's assume the murderer in this case is not from Alpha Centauri, but Sicily. Let's say we are not trying to prove that the killer is an extraterrestrial, but a Mafioso—are we ready to go to the DA? Are we ready to go, with this evidence, to the DA? What is he going to say? Have we got enough to go to trial and be confident of a win?"

Everybody turned to look at us. Dehan looked at me. I thought about it for a moment and stood.

"First of all, I can't speak for the DA. Maybe Darcel is a fan of *The X-Files*. I don't know her that well. But setting that to one side, it's not that simple, Colonel. Because we're talking about different burdens of proof. The burden of proof you need to convince a cop, or the DA, that the Mafia was behind a murder is actually pretty low." There was a small ripple of laughter. "But the burden of proof you need to convince a court of law that Robert De Niro whacked Joe Pesci in Tony's Ristorante on February fourteenth is very high. It is, as you said, beyond a reasonable doubt.

"What does that mean? What am I saying here? I'm saying that, if Joe Pesci winds up dead, shot six times, execution style, in Tony's Ristorante, I'm already pretty sure it was the Mob. I might be wrong, but I am personally convinced this was a Mob hit. However, to convict De Niro in a court of law, I need *proof*. I need the murder weapon, I need forensic evidence from ballistics, I need fingerprints, I need eyewitnesses who can personally identify De Niro. And above all I need not just a victim, but also a *particular person* I can attribute the murder to." I shrugged. "The difference is that I am looking for an Italian *individual*. You are trying to prove the Italians actually exist."

He smiled. "Fair point."

There was a lot of muttering and murmuring. After a moment, I added, "For what it's worth, if you were trying to prove, in a court of law, that those murders could only have been committed by . . . the 'Mafia,' I'd say you'd have the defense sweating and loosening their ties."

There was a fifteen-minute break, and for a short while the room was in mild uproar. People thronged around Colonel Hait and Donald Kirkpatrick and I scanned the room for Paul.

Dehan pointed, said, "He's there," and swung her long legs over the back of her chair to go after him.

I followed her through the crowd to where Paul was talking to a small man in sparkling eye shadow and a purple velvet cloak. She placed a hand on his shoulder and smiled, but it wasn't a particularly nice smile.

I said to the man in the cloak, "May we borrow him for a while?" and gently hustled Paul out to the corridor. The doors thudded behind us and suddenly it was very quiet.

He was looking from me to Dehan and back again. He looked worried. "Is there a problem?"

I shook my head. "No. We were just talking, and we have a few loose ends we'd like you to tie up for us. Maybe you could come in tomorrow and we could go over them with you?"

"Loose ends? Like what?"

I smiled. "Let's talk about it tomorrow. What time suits you?"

He looked more worried. "Nine a.m.?"

"Perfect."

The door opened and Kirkpatrick stepped out with his wife behind him. The agreeable smile had gone, replaced with his usual look of sour betrayal. He saw Paul and snapped, "There you are. I'm going to take the detectives to the small conference room. I need you to supervise the Q and A. Do you think you can manage that?"

"Of course." To us he said, "Excuse me," and went back inside.

Kirkpatrick said, "Follow me," and began to walk. He had a large bag hung around his shoulder. As I fell into step beside him, he extracted from it a cardboard box containing a videocassette. "Remember these?" He handed it to me. "It wasn't so long ago. They were replaced by digital cameras only twelve years ago, but it seems like another world. That's the original film, shot on the

Sunday night, over Soundview Park. I assume you will want to hang on to it as evidence, but I would like it back when you're done with it."

He pushed into a small conference room and Dehan, Jasmine, and I followed him in. There was a row of windows along one wall with slatted blinds drawn down, shutting out the night. A long table occupied the center of the floor with six chairs set around it. He turned to his wife and said, "Kill some of these lights, will you?"

As she did so, he pulled a laptop from his bag, opened it, and plugged a pen drive into one of the USB ports. He rattled at the keyboard and said, "Sit down, Detectives. This is a digital copy of exactly what you have on the videotape I have given you."

We sat, and he turned the laptop to face us, then stepped away with one hand behind his back, the other separating the slats of the blinds so he could gaze out the window at the darkness and the distant sparkle of anonymous lights.

The screen was black. Then it was suddenly filled with fuzzy, colored light that moved around while the cameraman tried to focus in on it. You could hear lots of excited voices. Some of them were screaming, others were asking, "*What the hell is it?*" The camera zoomed out, focused, and then began to zoom slowly in again. In the foreground you could see a throng of people. I guessed about forty or fifty, lining O'Brien Avenue, staring up at the sky. Many of them had umbrellas.

You could also make out the line of trees that fringed and concealed the park, so that it was impossible to tell if Danny was already there or not. Above the park, in the air, the shape of the UFO was not discernible. All you could see were bright red, blue, and yellow lights, and among them smaller lights of the same colors, which were flashing intermittently. It was hard to tell if the object was stable or not, because the camera was moving, so it seemed to dance around on the screen. But by freezing the image I was able to make a rough estimate of its size. I said to Dehan, "What do you think, six to ten feet across?"

She nodded.

Kirkpatrick said to the window, "The experts we submitted it to estimated eight, so you are in the same ballpark."

Dehan spoke half to herself. "Too small to carry a man or a woman."

I shrugged. "Assuming he was a full-size human."

She frowned at me, but before she could answer I pressed Play again. Loud screams erupted from the computer. What had triggered the screams was a sudden burst of red lasers, about six of them, that erupted from the belly of the craft toward the ground. Somebody expostulated, "*Holy shit!*"

Somebody else was shouting, "*It's an attack! Is it an attack? What the hell is going on? Is it an attack?*"

The lasers stopped and then erupted again. The bursts were repeated a total of six times, then the craft began to move away, out over the East River. It was hard to be precise, but I figured it had gone three or four hundred yards when there was a white flash and it vanished.

There were more screams and shouts, the camera searched the sky, there were more voices saying, "*It's gone! It's just gone, man!*" And the film ended.

I sat back in my chair, staring at the blank screen, thinking. I said, absently, "You showed this to the Feds?"

He was still peering out through the slats. "I contacted them and invited them to come and view it. They took it away, copied it, and returned it."

"Did they comment on it?"

He smiled, let go of the slats, and came to stand by the table. "They said it was clearly authentic, but it was impossible to see what it was." He sighed noisily. "What is clear, I think you'll agree, is that when it fires its lasers, it is right above where Danny's body was found."

I nodded. "Yes, that much is clear."

He stared at me from under his eyebrows. It struck me that his was an angry, bitter face. It was a face, I thought, that had been robbed and now wanted revenge. He said, suddenly, "We are at war, Detective Stone, only we don't know it. I don't know if the government knows it, or if there are people in the bureau or the CIA who know it. I hope so, but innocent people, like Danny, are being systematically abducted, mutilated, and killed, and as of today, we are defenseless against them."

I sighed and stood. "That's a lot of conclusions, Mr. Kirkpatrick. Maybe it's like me and the Mob." I gestured at the computer. "That is enough for you to know for sure that you are right in what you believe. But to prove it, in a court of law, or before a select committee, you need hard evidence. You need a weapon, fingerprints, DNA . . ." I shook my head. "What you have here is a compelling argument. But you do not have proof of anything, except that there were lights over Soundview Park the night Danny was found there."

He studied my face a moment, then looked away. "I am a scientist, Detective Stone, I know about evidence and proof. I was not intending to prove anything to you. I was simply hoping to open your eyes to what is happening. I hope I have done that, if only a little."

I held up the tape cassette. "Thank you for this. We'll be in touch."

Out in the corridor again, I saw Stuart and May Brown standing, holding paper cups of coffee and talking quietly to each other. I stared at Dehan a moment, thinking, then made my way toward them. She followed. Stuart looked up as we approached and half grimaced, half smiled. "Detectives, we didn't expect to see you here. We were just debating whether to go home."

I smiled blandly. "Subtle. No need, we are just leaving."

He closed his eyes a moment. "I didn't mean to be rude."

"Don't worry, we're used to it. I just wanted to ask you something. I keep hearing about how devoted Danny was to the subject of UFOs . . ."

Stuart nodded. "It was his life. I have no doubt, if he had

lived, he would have become one of the big names in the field. He had that kind of dedication."

I nodded. "That is certainly the impression I am getting. But I also keep hearing about how attractive he was to women."

May laughed out loud. There was an element of ridicule to it, but a lot of maternal pride too. I watched her and waited for her to stop. Dehan asked, "What's the joke?"

She smiled at Dehan and there was a hard glint in her eyes. "Don't take offense, honey, I'm on your side. I am just amused to see that the New York Police Department is as imaginative as ever in its investigation of crime."

My eyebrows told her I was surprised. "I didn't know you were a criminologist, Mrs. Brown. I thought you were a secondary school music teacher."

Her face became hostile.

I didn't let her answer. I turned to Stuart. "It would be very helpful for us to have a better understanding of Danny's romantic life. Did he have a girlfriend, was there anyone special . . ."

May started talking again. "What possible connection can that have with his . . ."

She didn't get any further. Dehan cut her dead. "Do you know who killed your son?"

May looked startled. "We are satisfied that . . ."

"I'm not asking you what species of being killed your son. I'm asking you if you know the name and identity of the individual who killed your son!"

"No, of course not . . ."

"It was never discovered, right?"

"No, but . . ."

"Did anybody ever investigate his love life before?"

"No . . ."

"So quit acting smart and answer the damned questions—honey."

She went puce.

I turned to Stuart. "What can you tell me about your son's love life, Mr. Brown?"

"Um . . . not a lot. It is true he was attractive to women. It wasn't unusual for him to have a woman stay the night. But there didn't seem to be anyone . . ."

He hesitated.

I said, "You're not one hundred percent sure about that, are you?"

He closed his eyes and shook his head. "It is nothing I can put my finger on, but I did have the feeling for a couple of weeks or so before he died that there might have been someone he was a little more serious about."

Dehan asked, "Someone he brought home?"

"No, that's just it. He didn't bring anyone home, which was unusual for him."

I raised an eyebrow. My mind was working faster than I could keep up with. "Someone he was taking to his van?"

He smiled. "It's possible. It was just a feeling."

I nodded. "Thank you. Enjoy the rest of the conference."

We stepped out of the hotel into the parking lot. It was floodlit by spindly, aluminum giants with glowing eyes that spread a depressing yellow light over several hundred cars, all of which observed us with dead, black windshields. Our heels made stark echoes across the silence as we crossed toward the Jag. Then Dehan stopped abruptly as I pulled the keys from my pocket. She looked up at the sky, but the sky was invisible, as were the stars, obscured by the glowing blanket of interference generated by the city lights. She spoke with her face upturned, trying to pierce that veil of light, to see into the dark.

"Why did they wait?" She looked at me. "If he transgressed some rule or law by not going to the glade, why didn't they zap him right there, at the campsite?"

"That was my question to you, remember?"

I opened the car, but she stayed, staring up, with the ghostly lamplight on her skin. "Now I'm asking you," she said quietly.

I smiled and shrugged. "Jack Alderman."

Now she looked at me and frowned. "Jack Alderman?"

"Sentenced to death in Georgia in 1975, and executed thirty-three years later."

She walked toward me and stood looking up into my face. "You mean, just because they are aliens doesn't mean they don't have procedures to follow? They had to seek authorization? Maybe there was an appeal? Rubber stamps...?"

"If, Dehan." I said, "*If* they are aliens. We have no idea what happened that night. This is all mind-blowing stuff, I agree, but none of it—*none* of it—so far, proves anything at all."

She puffed out her cheeks and blew, then leaned the top of her head against my chest. "Take me home," she said. "My head is going to explode."

TWELVE

She was peeling potatoes by the sink. I took a cold beer from the fridge and cracked it for her, then mixed myself a strong martini, dry. I took a long pull, felt myself start to relax, and started cutting the potatoes into French fries. I glanced at her. Her face was kind of rigid. She peeled and chopped some onion and garlic and threw them in a pan of oil with the potatoes. After that, she wrenched open the fridge and hauled out tomatoes, lettuce, avocado, cucumber, and, from a cupboard, a jar of artichoke hearts. Then she started making salad with enough aggression to take down Mike Tyson. When she had reduced the tomatoes to a bloody mess, she turned and stared at me with wide eyes and clenched jaw.

"We are going about this all wrong."

I shrugged with one shoulder. "I would have cut the tomatoes into chunks rather than make a puree."

"*Danny was not killed by aliens!*"

"As I have said to you before, statistics support that view."

"*But!*"

"But..."

"From trigger to execution..."

"You mean from the trance on Friday night to his death Sunday night?"

"There simply wasn't time to set up something this elaborate..."

"You said Paul might have been building up for months..."

"For petrol and drones! But we've seen it was much more elaborate than that! Something *this* elaborate..."

I sighed. "Okay..."

"That is..." She put her long index finger on my chest. "There wasn't time for people with the resources of Paul or Jane to set it up."

"Jane?"

She looked surprised. "Sure, she has as much motive as Paul."

"Interesting. But you are saying not Jane because she hadn't the resources."

"Yeah, but my point is, I am excluding the damned aliens!"

"So our question, you are saying, should be, who, exclusively among humans, had the resources?"

"Yes!"

"And your suggestion is...?"

She stared at me for a long moment. "Are you taking me seriously?"

"Yes." I pulled the salad bowl over and started making a salad that didn't look like the Texas Chainsaw Massacre. "But while you tell me your thoughts, open the wine and put the steaks on."

She walked away and after a moment I heard the cork pop. Then the fridge opened and closed, and she came and stood next to me while the griddle got hot. She said, "The Feds."

I stopped dead and turned to stare at her. "The Feds? Dehan, do you realize what you are saying?"

"Of course I do."

I shook my head. "No. It doesn't make sense. They might, at a real stretch, break the rules to eliminate a terrorist, somebody the director deemed a real threat, but Danny Brown? Besides, that culture hasn't existed in the bureau since Hoover."

She held up her hands. "Okay, okay, okay, maybe not the Feds, but some department acting on information supplied by the Feds."

I stared at her for a long time. I had a bad feeling. Past her shoulder I could see the griddle beginning to smoke. I sighed. "Let's get the meat on."

She sprinkled coarse salt on them, slung them on the iron, and they hissed and caught fire. I took the salad to the table, checked the French fries, and started to spoon them onto the plates. We didn't talk again till we were sitting at the table and I was pouring the wine.

I watched her cut into her steak and was momentarily hypnotized by the trace of blood that trickled across her plate and mixed with the oil from the salad. She stuffed the piece in her mouth and watched me while she chewed. She said, with her mouth full, "Come on, Stone, we both know there are departments in the White House and the Pentagon that not even the president is aware of."

I stuffed an excess of fries and steak into my mouth and said, "Bumph, oy, eehang?" She frowned. I swallowed and drained half my glass of wine. "But why, Dehan? Why would the federal government want to assassinate Danny Brown? It's nuts. Leave aside for the moment the effort and expense of such an elaborate hit. Why would they want to kill *him*, of all people? A twenty-year-old geek! They have a hundred terrorists, Islamic and domestic, they could go after. Why Danny Brown, who is not a threat to anybody?"

She pointed at me with her fork. "But what if he was?"

I spread my hands. "How?"

She wagged the fork and narrowed her eyes. "We have been focusing on the relationship between Jane, Danny, and Paul, thinking of a sexual motive for his murder. But what else happened that night, Stone?"

I sighed, ate, and thought. "The trance..."

She shook her head. "That is still in the sexual motivation. It triggered Jane's jealousy and Paul's. Before that. What were they talking about? What were they excited about? Why were they still up when everybody else had gone to bed?"

"The lights they had seen, and the signals Don said were not naturally occurring."

"Stone, what if the equipment Don had developed allowed them to stumble on a classified military research program? It is not so far-fetched. There was a lot of high-tech R and D going on at that time. They *did* see something that night, and they did hear something, and . . ."

"We don't know that. We only know they believe they did."

"But that very weekend Danny dies in very bizarre circumstances. Circumstances that so far neither of us has been able to explain. Circumstances that require *resources*!"

We ate in silence for a while. We drained our glasses and I refilled them. Then she said, "You have to ask yourself, Stone. I mean, just put the idea of aliens out of your mind for a moment. Let's have a reality check. If you eliminate the alien hypothesis, you *have* to ask yourself, why would his killer make it look like he was killed by aliens? And also, who had the resources to do that at such short notice?"

I nodded. "Those are probably the most important questions we could ask right now."

She spread her hands. "It is the ultimate red herring. As long as you are looking for aliens, you are not looking for a person. It's like what you said to the colonel. They are trying to prove the existence of a species, instead of looking for the individual responsible for the murder."

I nodded, a lot. "Dehan, I think you have put your finger on it. That is precisely it, isn't it. The ultimate red herring."

She leaned across the table. "So who has the resources? The CIA, the Pentagon, Military Intelligence. They detect that somebody is tracking one of their experimental vehicles. There were a number in development in the '90s. They detect their position, track them, and . . . zap!"

I grunted and tackled my steak again.

"If you're right, Dehan, and there is no doubt you might be, we have as much chance of getting our man as Donald Trump has of winning Mr. Congeniality 2018. Let's stay focused and take baby steps. You nailed the question: What would make the killer want to make it look as though an alien killed him? That's a question for us, and tomorrow we have Paul coming in, and our question for him is, why didn't he tell us that he and Jane had a row over Danny, and split up the night before Danny died? So far, Carmen, that is still the most compelling motive we have. We have motive and we have opportunity, which we did not have yesterday, all we are lacking is means."

She sighed. "Yeah, you're right, motive and opportunity. But man, means . . ." She shook her head. "It's easily said."

We finished our meal, and while I washed up, she made coffee and poured a couple of generous measures of Bushmills. We took them out to the backyard and sat on the swing seat with a small table in front of us. She curled up and nestled next to me, under my arm.

"I'm an alien, Stone."

"Are you? I have wondered at times. It's that green tint of your skin."

"I'm serious. I don't mean I'm from another planet, I mean I don't belong."

"I know what you mean."

"You're the same, but you're better at pretending than I am." She sipped her whiskey and stared into her glass for a bit. "I use you."

I didn't know how to answer, so I waited.

"I use you to communicate with *them*. If you're not there, I end up being rude or blunt. That's why people say I have an attitude." She looked up at my face and smiled. "If somebody is being stupid I'll say, 'You're being stupid,' but if you're there you'll say, 'Have you thought about it this way? Or that way?'" She stopped and gazed at the dim glimmer of the stars. "I guess what I am trying to say is, you help me to be in this world."

"I'm glad," I said. "It wouldn't be much of a world without you."

She nestled the top of her head into my chin. Her hair smelled of apples. Somewhere, out in the wilds of the Bronx, an owl in a tree hooted, a single star winked, and the vast, infinite sky stretched and yawned. Then, I swear, it gave a self-satisfied smile.

PAUL LOOKED NERVOUS. More than nervous, he looked unhappy. I smiled at him regretfully. It was a smile that was designed, subtly, to make him feel more nervous and unhappy than he did already.

I said, "We spoke to Jane Harrison."

He gave a single, upward nod.

I went on, "She told us what happened on the Friday and the Saturday."

He stared down at his huge fists on the table and chewed his lip.

I waited. When he didn't say anything, I said, "I'm giving you the opportunity to fill out the statement you already gave us. You must be aware, Paul, that all the bits you left out cast you in a pretty bad light right now."

He took a deep breath and closed his eyes as he blew out. It was a very eloquent gesture. He opened his eyes and stared for a long time at Dehan. "You would not believe how sick I am of hearing everybody talk about what a great guy Danny was. You know? I loved that guy. Seriously. I loved him more than a brother. Especially before..."

He stopped dead.

Dehan said, "Before what?"

"Okay, I'll say it. Before Jane came on the scene." He sighed again. "I was pretty serious about her. I was ready to marry her.

What is it with people, huh?" He looked at me as though I might have an answer to his unspoken question. "We never fall in love with the people who are good for us. You noticed that? We always fall in love with the people who are going to hurt us. I knew! I *knew* she was in love with Danny. But she couldn't have him, because Danny was in love with fuckin' . . ." He made a gesture with his open hand, like he was pointing at some imaginary TV screen. "Dana Scully! That was his ideal woman. And . . ." He turned to Dehan. "Forgive me if I am sexist, and maybe you are completely different, but in my experience, women cannot resist a guy who is unattainable. And Danny—he was straight, he had his biological needs, sex was fun, but he was one hundred percent emotionally unobtainable! That was it. Do not go any deeper than that! And every damn woman he knew wanted to have a ride in his damned van. You know he had this special van where he screwed chicks, right? Sorry."

He made a fist and softly pounded the table. "I shouldn't talk about him like that. He was my friend and I swear to God I loved him like a brother. But he was a womanizer. That's God's truth." He crossed himself and kissed his thumb. "It's God's truth. Other men are womanizers and they are obsessed with women. Not him. He didn't even try. He didn't even *know*. It was just like, 'Who am I gonna fuck tonight?' And there would be three or four chicks all waiting in line in case he chose them. You know? And in the end it just got, boring. I got bored. I got tired of always being in his fucking shadow."

Dehan asked, "So if she was in love with him . . ."

He spread his hands, like it was obvious. "She couldn't have him, so she took me. I was his best friend. Second best. You can't afford the Mercedes S-Class so you buy the A-Class. You can't afford an apartment on Madison Avenue, but you buy one in a cheaper part of Manhattan. I was his best friend. She couldn't have him, so she took me instead."

"That's pretty harsh."

"It's also true."

"Must have made you mad."

"Yeah!" He flopped back in his chair. "Yeah, it made me mad. It made me mad at her and it made me mad at him. I was mad at her for being a cheap hypocrite whose feelings . . . whose *love*, was so fuckin' *shallow*, you know what I'm saying? Was so fuckin' *shallow* she didn't care who she was giving it to. Who was so lacking in compassion and empathy, that she didn't care what it did to me that she was gonna screw my best friend, just so long as she got what she wanted."

Dehan frowned and raised an eyebrow. "How do you know she was going to screw him?"

"C'mon! I'm not stupid! As soon as Don tells Jasmine she's not going to the glade, Jane is all over Danny like a fuckin' rash: 'Let's you and me go! We can't let this opportunity go! It's too good! Let's you and me go, Danny!'" He shrugged. "What are they gonna do up there in the glade? Count the fuckin' stars?"

I nodded. "But Don put a stop to that. He was already concerned, even back then, about the cases of human mutilation."

"Yeah. He said we all go or nobody goes. As it turned out, he was right. But I had already made up my mind by then, I was through with Jane."

"What happened next, Paul?"

He thought for a bit before answering. "I let Jane know I was mad. I let Danny know too. I didn't care anymore if she screwed Danny or not, but I was damned sure I was going to break up with her before she did. She was not going to screw another guy while she was my girlfriend. You know what I am saying? You don't do that. That is a deep lack of respect for your partner. So we slept three or four hours, till just after dawn, and went back to Don's place."

"But things continued to get worse with you, Jane, and Danny."

He shrugged. "Danny knew something was wrong, and he was kind of backing away from Jane a bit. But at the same time, he wasn't really interested. He had no time for that problem. He was buzzing with what we had seen that night. He was real curious about the signals we had picked up. Him and Don, they were convinced that we had hard evidence of the presence of alien ships in Earth's atmosphere. What he did not need was Jane causing problems in the group."

I leaned back in my chair, trying to visualize the scene. "How was Don taking all this?"

He smiled. "He was oblivious, man. He had no idea. Him and Danny." He shook his head. "They lived in a different world, on a different plane." He shrugged. "We packed up and went back to Don's place. But Jane wouldn't let up. Right away, even over breakfast, all her conversation is for Danny. She's making comments about his van, kind of teasing him, messing with him. It was humiliating."

Dehan shook her head, like she would not tolerate something like that. "I can't imagine how that made you feel."

He looked her straight in the eye. "I'll tell you how it made me feel. It made me feel like killing her. Taking my katana and cutting her fucking head off."

THIRTEEN

THERE WAS A HEAVY SILENCE IN THE INTERROGATION room. After a moment, Dehan said to him, "Paul, are you aware that the statement you just made incriminates you and makes you a suspect in our investigation?"

He smiled down at his hand and gave a soft snort. After a moment, he raised an eyebrow at her. "What? You're telling me you hadn't already decided I was jealous and had a motive for killing Danny? I'm not stupid, Detective Dehan. I know why you asked me to come in this morning." He shook his head. "In my moments of rage, I wanted to kill Jane for lying to me, for pretending to love me when she didn't, for putting me in the way of all that pain and disappointment when, if she had just been honest from the start, it would not have been necessary. I did, I wanted to kill her for that. But Danny?" He shrugged. "Danny, I wanted to give him two good smacks around the head and tell him to wake the fuck up! Stop fuckin' flirting with every fuckin' woman you meet, man! He doesn't realize it, but when he is playing his little games, to him it's funny, but he is hurting people! That's not nice. It's not respectful. I wanted to slap him around the head, but I did not want to kill him." He gave a small, private laugh. "Bottom line, he meant more to me than she did. The fuckin' son of a bitch."

I studied him through narrowed eyes, trying to see if he was a good actor or if he was being honest. I decided I couldn't tell and said, "So what happened next?"

"What happened next? It was one of the longest days of my life. Don was a very different kind of man back then. He was a really nice guy. He was open, generous, polite . . ." He looked at me and laughed a big laugh, pointing at me. "You wouldn't believe it, huh? He's a real fuckin' grouch now. He reminds me of that guy on *The Muppets*." He turned to Dehan. His laughter was infectious. "You know the one? He lives in a trash can. Don reminds me of him. But he didn't used to be like that. He was a nice guy and he had been looking forward to that party. We'd brought beer, meat to barbeque, wine." He shook his head. "The truth is most people were pretty freaked out by what had happened. But it's also true that Jane . . ." He shrugged. "And, the truth be told, Danny too, they were bringin' the mood down. It was hard to ignore them, and everybody was feeling bad for me and trying not to show it. The whole thing was embarrassing."

I scratched my chin. "So, if I am hearing you right, by the afternoon Danny had started to join in with Jane."

He nodded. "Yeah. I have to admit that. He didn't mean anything by it. But by the afternoon he was playing along, flirting back. I had taken Jane aside and asked her to have the minimum respect of not humiliating me in front of all my friends, you know? But she just dismissed me and told me to get a life, or words to that effect. So I thought, yeah. She's right. You know? Never a truer word spoken. It was time for me to get a life, a life without her in it. Make room for a woman who would love and like me, and *respect* me—not some other guy.

"So right there, in front of everybody, I went up to Danny and I pointed at him and I said, 'I am real mad at you. This is not how you treat a friend. I would never, *never,* do this to you. And Monday, you and me are gonna talk about this!' Then I turned to her and I said, 'I'm going home, I brought you in my car, so I will take you home in my car if you want me to. Otherwise you can go in Danny's fuckin' fuck-mobile!' And I saw how she looked at him, like asking, you know, 'Can I come home with you?' But Danny was real upset. Our friendship meant a lot to both of us, and he was not happy. Fuckin' Jane was nothing to him. So he frowns at me and says, 'I don't know what you're mad about, bro . . .'"

He stopped suddenly and I could see tears in his eyes. His jaw muscles were bunching and when he spoke again he sounded like he had a bad cold. "He says, 'I don't know what I've done, Paul, but whatever it is, I'm sorry, man. We can talk now.' He said that, 'We can talk now, we go outside and we can talk this through.' But I was too mad and I said I was leaving. I just wanted to break up with Jane and get it over with. So he looks at her and frowns and shakes his head. She asks him, outright, 'You want me to stay?' and he looks at her like she's crazy, and he says, 'No! He's your boyfriend. Go with him and sort it out!'"

Dehan asked, "So everybody left about the same time?"

"I guess. Danny said he was staying for a bit to speak with Don. Jane and I didn't talk all the way back. It was the longest drive of my life. Finally, I dropped her at her place. It was her parents' place back then. I remember it like it was yesterday. I had been really in love with her. I was going to marry her, for Christ's sake! You know? And as she was opening the door . . ." He shook his head, still incredulous after twenty years. "She was just going to get out of the car and go into her house, without saying anything. But I stopped her. I said, 'I got to tell you something before you get out of the car.' She says, 'Can't it wait? I'm tired.' I said, 'No, because I am probably never going to talk to you again.' So she goes kind of frozen, like she's shocked. I said, 'You are a shallow, selfish, unfeeling bitch. You used me and you discarded me with no consideration for my feelings. You were willing to destroy me without compassion, just so you could play your little game with Danny.' Then I told her, 'Get out of my car and get out of my life. I never want to see you again.' She got out and she had the *gall*—the sheer, fuckin' *gall*—to run into her house crying! Can you believe that?" He sat staring at the wall, shaking his head. "Man, I haven't talked about this for years. It brings it all back."

Dehan said, "That was pretty brutal. What did you do next?"

"I continued on my way and went home. There I went to bed and I am ashamed to say I cried myself to sleep. The next day I started drinking around lunchtime and I don't think I sobered up for a week."

"Can anyone confirm that?"

He shrugged. "I honestly can't remember, Detective Stone." He smiled at me. I was surprised to see that it was not an unsympathetic smile. "I don't mean to be funny, but I don't honestly feel I need an alibi. Because there was no way on God's green Earth that I was capable of inventing whatever it was that incinerated Danny and cut off his head and his feet. Could I have cut off his head and his feet with my katana?" He nodded. "For sure. Could I have incinerated him and placed him there in the park, and arranged for a space probe to fly over and fire its damned lasers at him?" He shook his head and smiled. "Nah. No way. That's out of my league. I wish you luck. I'd like to catch whoever did it, especially if Don is wrong and you are right, and it was a person who killed him. But I honestly don't think it was. This is one case you are never going to solve, unless you start looking somewhere else."

Dehan heaved a big sigh and absently tied her hair behind her neck. When she was done, she said, "Can you tell us any more about the signals that Don picked up, or the thing you saw flying in the sky? I noticed he doesn't say much about it in his book."

He made a face. "Not really. The signals I didn't understand at all. He said there were too many random variations for it to be of a natural origin. The images, he had a special camera focused on a sector of the sky to the southwest of our position. He had special lenses and software that allowed him to connect the camera to the computer, and then on the screen you could see these objects appear and disappear, flying across the sky just the way he described them."

"Did he record it?"

"Yeah, he recorded it on his computer."

"What did he do with the recordings, do you know?"

He shrugged. "You'd have to ask him, but I think he contacted the FBI and the Air Force and offered them sight of what he had recorded. I don't know what came of that. He never told anybody."

Dehan glanced at me. I had no more questions, but I was reluctant to let him go. I wanted to go over everything he had said again. I had a gut feeling he had said something that I had missed. It was nagging at my mind, but I couldn't pin it down. They were both watching me, waiting. I tried to run through the whole conversation, focusing on what he had said, on what he had told us, but I couldn't nail it. It was in there, some small comment he'd made, but I couldn't find it. Finally, I shook my head and spread my hands.

"Thank you, Paul. You have been very helpful."

"We're done? I can go?"

"Sure, of course."

I stood and saw him to the door. There he stopped a moment and looked into my face. "It wasn't Jane, you know. I didn't mean to suggest that Jane did it either." He shrugged. "I don't see how anybody could have done it."

I nodded. "I know, Paul. Thanks."

He left, and I watched him go down the stairs. Then I went back into the interrogation room, closed the door, and went and rested my ass on the table. Dehan was still sitting. I crossed my arms and looked down at her.

"Did anything in what he said strike you as significant?"

She thought for a while before answering, then kind of shrugged with her eyebrows. "He struck me as sincere. His story seems very believable. And it is hard to imagine him getting back and in just a few hours putting together that elaborate plan. There must be a thousand simpler, more satisfying ways he could have killed him, and still got away with it."

I grunted. "Yeah. No. It wasn't that."

"Also, it rang true that he was mad at her, not Danny."

I shook my head. "There was something he said. It's stuck in my brain, like when you get something stuck in your teeth, but I'm not sure what it was. He said something..."

She screwed up her eyes. "You think it might have been her, Stone? What's that quote?"

"'Hell hath no fury like a woman scorned.' It's possible. But it doesn't get us very far."

Her face had suddenly taken on a strange expression, like slow shock. "You know what her job is, Stone?"

I frowned. "Uh, yeah, she told me, she's a TV producer. That was why she was able to come in and see us in the morning, because she has an odd schedule..." I trailed off. "Oh..."

She nodded several times, staring at me. "Yeah, oh indeed... Stone, if anyone has the skill to set up an elaborate *production* like this one, it would be someone in TV or the movies."

"Maybe. We need to find out exactly what aspect of production she's involved in, and, more to the point, what she was doing twenty years ago. She works for NBC. Get on the phone to them. Keep it confidential, I don't want her to know we're looking at her yet."

"What are you going to do?"

"I'm going to play back this interview and listen to it. There is something Paul said, Dehan, some passing comment..."

But just as I was saying it, my cell rang.

"Stone."

"Detective Stone, this is Special Agent Smith, of the Federal Bureau of Investigation. I was wondering if you and Detective Carmen Dehan could come down to the field office for a talk."

I stared at Dehan a moment. "Yeah. Of course. What's this about?"

"Your current investigation into the death of Danny Brown."

"You have information that could help us?"

"Why don't we discuss that when you're here, Detective? Say, in half an hour?"

"Make that forty-five minutes. We'll see you then. Thanks for calling." I hung up before he could answer and looked at Dehan. "The bureau. Agent Smith."

She raised an eyebrow. "Seriously? What's the bet his partner is Agent Brown?"

I nodded. "Let's go."

FOURTEEN

Agent Smith did not have his name on the door of his small, anonymous office. Neither did he look the way he sounded. His voice had somehow suggested someone who had had all his compassion and humanity ruthlessly trained out of him. But to look at, Agent Smith looked like somebody's uncle. He was of average height, slim, with a soft, round face and balding, curly blond hair. He wore round glasses, which added to the soft roundness of his face. But in spite of his uncle-ish look, he did not have a smile.

He rose as we stepped in and came around the desk to shake our hands. There was another man there who also stood. He did smile. He wore a suit, a black moustache, and tightly curled black hair. Agent Smith spoke as we shook. "Detectives, thank you for coming in. This is Agent Brown. I know how busy you must be, so we appreciate your taking the time."

We sat and they sat. I noticed there were no papers on his desk, no jar with pens in it, and no photos of his nieces and nephews on the desk, or the bookcase. In fact, there was no bookcase either. He said, "I'll come straight to the point. Agent Bernie Hirschfield passed on your inquiry to us. Do you mind telling us exactly what your interest is in this case?"

I stared at him and drew breath to answer but Dehan was already talking. "What kind of a question is that? Our interest? It was a homicide committed within the jurisdiction of the Forty-Third Precinct. It wasn't solved at the time, and we are in charge of cold cases. That's our interest, Agent Smith."

Smith blinked at her but aside from that showed no expression. Brown smiled. "It is simply," he said, "that we were surprised at its resurfacing after all these years, and we wondered why."

I answered before Dehan could get in. "Purely routine, Agent Brown. We have been working through the cold cases, and this one came up. That's what happens with cold cases. I am not going to inquire as to why you are interested that we are interested. Presumably you are doing your job and you have your reasons, just as we do. But what I am going to inquire about is whether you did, in fact, visit some of the witnesses in the original case."

They looked at each other. Smith nodded at Brown and turned to me. "We did visit some of the witnesses. I'm not sure 'witness' is the right word, as it seems that nobody, in fact, witnessed the murder. But we did visit some of Daniel's friends and family."

Dehan crossed one of her long legs over the other and coughed. "A homicide within New York is not in the bureau's jurisdiction. What made you look into it?"

Brown smiled his bland, friendly smile again. "It wasn't the *fact* of the homicide, Detective Dehan, but the *nature* of the homicide."

"The fact that there was an apparent UFO involved, or the similarity with the cattle mutilations in the Midwest?"

He didn't hesitate. "Both. The official position of the bureau on UFOs is that we are not aware of any extraterrestrial presence either on this planet or within the United States, but we certainly don't discount the possibility. That would be absurd, when our own National Aeronautics and Space Administration is actively seeking out life on other planets!" He laughed. "Naturally, we were aware of the homicide and of the UFO over the park. So when it emerged that the local police were unable to solve the case, we went and asked a few questions."

I nodded. "The consensus amongst the people you spoke to, in particular Donald Kirkpatrick, is that they were instructed not to talk about what had happened."

Smith smiled for the first time. It wasn't what you'd call warm, but it was amused.

"We obviously didn't do a very good job of scaring them into silence then, did we?" He looked over at Brown and added, "We should get the boys over at the CIA to give us men in black lessons." They both laughed. Then Smith turned back to me and pressed the point home. "After all, he went on to publish a book that sold well over a million copies. I think if the bureau wanted to silence somebody, Detective Stone, we could do it a little more effectively than that. However, despite what popular fiction may have you believe, we do not actually indulge in that kind of activity. We leave that to the boys at Langley."

They laughed again and Agent Brown said, "No, we can only speculate as to Mr. Kirkpatrick's motives for claiming that we tried to silence him, but the fact is that we had no reason to do so. It has, nonetheless, given a definite boost to his sales over the years. If you look at his website, the alleged attempts by the bureau to silence him are quite prominent in his . . ." He hesitated a moment. "In his sales pitch."

I nodded. "So are you telling me that the FBI had no interest in the case, and made no attempt to silence the witnesses?"

Smith answered. "That is exactly what we are telling you. Putting it bluntly, Detective, we don't mind Kirkpatrick cashing in on a little post-*X-Files* paranoia about the bureau, but we don't want the NYPD running away with the idea that we go around threatening their witnesses."

"Okay, well, we appreciate that."

"But while you're here, off the record, may we inquire whether you have developed a theory as to who killed Daniel, and how?"

I studied Smith's face. It was an inscrutable mask, and you could tell he had spent years perfecting it. I turned to Brown. His smile had that same impenetrable quality. I turned back to Smith. "Why do you ask?"

He nodded a few times, and just for a second his mask slipped and he looked worried. "In case it's something the bureau does need to have a look at."

I thought about it for a moment, then shook my head. "No, I don't think so. If we are leveling with each other, the case is baffling, and we have considered a number of possibilities that are pretty 'out there,' but for now I don't think this is anything that need concern the bureau."

He nodded. "Okay, but if you do come across anything that might, for example, affect national security, please contact me or Agent Brown directly." He slid a card across the desk to Dehan, and Brown pulled a card from his wallet and handed it to me. "Any time of the night or day," he said. "Be sure to call us."

I glanced at Dehan, then nodded at Smith and Brown. "We'll do that. Thanks for answering our questions."

We stood, shook hands, and left.

Out on Broadway, we were assaulted by the heat and the avalanche of traffic and people and noise that flows eternally among those canyons of steel. We started walking toward the car and Dehan pulled out her cell and said, "That wasn't their office, and those weren't their names."

"I know."

She went on talking as she dialed with her thumb. "They just wanted to find out if we'd found anything, and fob us off. They must think we're stupid."

I nodded.

She put the phone to her ear. "Yeah, get me the number for NBC Personnel . . ." She glanced at me. "Thirty Rock, Sensei."

By the time we got there, we had the name of the producer of the show that Jane was working on, and she was happy to grant us ten quick minutes if we could get there right away. I wondered if ten quick minutes passed faster than ten slow minutes, but before I could give it much thought, we had arrived.

We found Elizabeth Anderson in a large, messy room, through a double door that had a plastic plaque on it that read *Night of the Stalker*. She was at the head of a table with seven writers sitting around it shouting ideas at each other. They went silent and turned to stare at us as we stepped in. We held up our badges. I said, "Elizabeth Anderson?"

She stood and pointed at a door over on one side. "Come into my office." As we approached, she turned back to the table. "Gerry, run with the mass suicide idea. But is it a priest or priestess? Gimme ten."

She pushed through the office door and we went in after her. She planted her ass on the edge of her desk and crossed her arms. She didn't invite us to sit. "I'm on the clock. What can I do for you?"

I gave her my deadest expression, counted slowly to three, and said, "We're on a homicide investigation. The clock can wait. Jane Harrison works with you?"

"Yeah. She's in production. Is she in trouble?"

"What is the nature of her work, exactly?"

She sighed. "It's technical. It's hard to explain exactly."

Dehan said, "In general terms that a dumb cop would understand."

"She works with technicians, mainly IT guys, integrating special effects sequences into the main narrative of the story."

I frowned. "So she's in special effects?"

She shook her head. "No, no, it's not like that anymore. Special effects are almost entirely computer-generated these days. What she does is work with the team that creates the special effects, and she then makes sure those sequences work in the overall context of the story."

Dehan grunted. "But to do that she would need some kind of understanding of how special effects work."

"Sure. And she has that. She's been in the business for twenty years, and she started out in special effects before they became exclusively CGI."

"And that would have been mainly horror, sci-fi . . ."

"Yeah, that kind of thing."

"How come she's not in today?"

"She phoned in sick."

I frowned. "Does she do that often?"

"No. Never. It must be bad, she didn't call in herself, got her friend to call."

"What friend?"

Now she looked irritated. "What am I? Her mom? How should I know what friend? A friend. I guess she has friends!"

"Did you take the call?"

"Yeah, I took it. But I don't know her friends. We work together."

"Man or a woman?"

"A woman! Are we done now? Do I need to sack her or not?"

I shook my head. "You don't need to sack her. Thanks for your help, and good luck with the mass suicide. I hope it works out for you."

"Yeah, funny, man. Thanks."

We rode the elevator down in silence and stepped out onto the plaza. Dehan drew breath, but I held up my hand. People jostled past us. "The immediate, obvious thing is that either Jane killed Danny using the skills she learned working in special effects or Paul killed him using the techniques that he had gleaned from talking to his fiancée. They both had motive and opportunity, and possibly the means—at least in theory."

She scowled at me. "That's what I was going to say. Also, remember that Danny's dad told us he had the impression Danny might be getting serious about somebody? If that somebody was Jane, it gives Paul an even more powerful motive. They argue in the car and Jane comes out with it. 'I've been seeing him regularly for the last two weeks!' You can imagine the scenario."

I stuck my hands in my pockets and we started to stroll back toward the car. I chewed my lip. "I can and I can't," I said, unhelpfully. "I can also see a scenario where Danny and Jane have been getting serious and Danny tells her it has to stop because he feels bad about his 'bro' Paul. And I can *also* see a scenario where Jane comes on to him and he tells her he is getting serious about some woman we know nothing about."

"True."

"A woman who somehow reminds him of Dana Scully, a committed ufologist, a bit mysterious . . ."

We had reached the car, and I walked around to the driver's side and leaned on the roof. She leaned on the opposite side and smiled at me. It was a nice smile.

"We are missing something, Carmen. It's driving me nuts. It's buzzing around in my head. Something Paul said." I opened the door. "Let's go and see how ill Jane really is and why she took the day off work. Maybe it will come to me on the way."

She climbed in after me and the doors slammed like two gunshots in the plaza. She gave me an odd look. "You don't believe she's ill?"

I shook my head. "And I want to know who phoned for her."

She frowned. "You think she's done a runner?"

"Maybe. Let's find out."

FIFTEEN

As we cruised up Madison Avenue it dawned on me that we had never been to Jane's house. I frowned and looked at Dehan. She had her elbow out the window and her hair all over her face. Two of me frowned back at me from her shades.

"Where does she live?"

"Castle Hill Avenue, across the creek from Donald Kirkpatrick."

I narrowed my eyes, trying to visualize it. "Across the creek? To the east?"

She smiled. "Only way to get across that creek is by going east, Sensei."

And then it began to dawn on me. My mind reached back, recalling what Paul had said. Dehan was watching me.

"What is it?"

"Paul. He said . . ." I chewed my lip, reaching for the words, trying to grasp them and hold them. "He said he drove Jane home . . ."

She nodded. "Yeah. He was a gentleman. He drove her there so . . ."

"No, no. How did he phrase it? He said . . ." I looked at her a moment, then at the long stream of traffic ahead. "He said it was the longest drive of his life..."

"Yeah, you're right. I noticed that and I thought it was odd. Donald's house to Jane's is maybe a mile and a half."

"But then he said something else."

She pushed her sunglasses up on her head, like a medieval visor, closed her eyes, and rested her head back, speaking like an android. "He laid it on the line for her. He told her she was a shallow, selfish bitch who used him and discarded him with no consideration for his feelings. Then he said she was willing to destroy him without pity, or compassion, just so she could have her little game with Danny. Then he told her to get out of his life."

I nodded. "That's right, then she got out of the car and he said she had the gall to run into the house crying. Then..." I looked at her and raised a finger. "Dehan, then you asked him what he did next, and he said, verbatim, and I quote, 'I continued on my way and went home...' It could be a trivial detail, Dehan, but I think..."

I went quiet, running through the possibilities in my mind, seeing the sequence of events. Dehan watched me awhile, shrugged, and spread her hands. "What, for crying out loud?"

"They weren't at Don's house."

"What are you talking about?"

"*God!*" I thumped the steering wheel. "I have been so *stupid*! Of course they weren't at Don's house!"

Dehan was shaking her head. "You lost me, Stone. Clue me in."

"Wait!" I began to accelerate. After a moment, I said, "Paul told us he has always lived in the same neighborhood. All of them! They have all always lived in the same damned place. Paul lives at the western end of Seward Avenue, near the top of Soundview Park, north and west of Don's house. Jane lives in the opposite direction, south and west of Don, but only a half hour's walk away. So why would Paul say, A, it was the longest drive of his life and, B, that he 'continued on his way'? *This*, this is what has been bugging me. Something else he said: he said they packed up the camp and went back to Don's place, and then, over breakfast, um . . ." I snapped my fingers, trying to remember. "'. . . even over breakfast, all her conversation was for Danny. She was making comments about his van, kind of teasing him . . .'"

We were speeding over the bridge. She was shaking her head. "Okay, it's odd . . . but, so what? What does it mean?"

I looked at her. "They packed up the camp, on Macomb Mountain, then they had breakfast at Don's? That's got to be two hundred or two hundred and fifty miles as the crow flies. That has to be four or five hours' drive." I shook my head. "How could I be so stupid?"

"So . . ." She frowned. "So they have a cabin up there . . . ?"

I nodded. "Yeah, they have a cabin up there."

She was silent for ten minutes, staring through the windshield. Finally, she said, "This is important . . . ?"

I nodded again and slowed to come off the Bruckner Boulevard. "If I am right, it blows the whole damned thing open."

She pulled her shades over her eyes as I accelerated down Castle Hill toward the creek. The tires complained as I braked outside her house, spun the wheel, and pulled into her drive, blocking her garage door. As we climbed out, Dehan made a grimace at me. "Sensei, I confess, I don't know what's going on."

I shook my head. "Later."

I hammered on the door and rang the bell. There was silence inside the house. I tried to peer through the window, but the drapes were drawn. I turned to Dehan. "I'm going to cover the front. Take the path, have a look 'round the back. See if the kitchen door is open."

She disappeared down the concrete path and I called Jane's telephone, tried the bell again, hammered some more on the door. Nothing. After a couple of minutes, Dehan reappeared, shaking her head. "Kitchen door is locked, all the drapes are drawn. You want to tell me what's on your mind?"

I chewed my lip at her. "We need to get inside."

A woman's voice called to us from the road.

"Can I help you?"

She was in her forties, in expensive jeans and a silk blouse. She had her shades on her head and her keys in her hand. Two doors up, I could see her SUV in a driveway with the trunk open. There were bags of shopping in the trunk and in the doorway.

"Are you a friend of Jane Harrison's?"

She smiled, but it was more courteous than friendly. "Who are you?"

I showed her my badge. "I'm Detective John Stone. This is my partner, Detective Dehan. We urgently need to talk to Jane. Do you know where she is?"

She looked surprised.

Before she could answer I said, "Was it you who phoned her in sick at work?"

"I haven't seen Jane since yesterday evening. She has a pretty chaotic schedule sometimes. I saw she was home and I came over. We had coffee and talked. She seemed fine." She hesitated a moment. "She did say she'd been invited to some kind of reunion, but she wasn't going to go."

Somewhere in the back of my mind an alarm bell went off. "This could be very important, Ms. . . ."

"Garrido, Olga Garrido."

"What kind of reunion? Where? Anything you can remember . . ."

She looked distressed. "Oh, gosh! Um . . . She said it was old friends she hadn't seen for a long time. She didn't seem keen, said they were a bit weird. An old boyfriend. But it was like midweek and she had work, so she wasn't going to go. I have a morning job. I've just got in . . ."

"Okay, thank you, Ms. Garrido. Go back to your house."

"Is she okay?"

"We'll take care of this."

She went back toward her SUV, glancing at us over her shoulder. I took my Swiss Army knife from my pocket and selected the small screwdriver, then examined the lock to see if it had been picked. It hadn't, so I photographed it, then rammed the screwdriver in the keyhole, fiddled around for a bit till the lock gave, and eased open the door. I looked back at Dehan. She had her weapon in her hands. I called out, "Jane! This is Detectives Stone and Dehan!"

There was only the oppressive silence. I gestured with my head at the living room and moved toward the kitchen-diner at the back. As I inched my way in, I heard the living room door creak behind me. Soft light filtered through the drapes over the sink. The big, silver fridge was humming softly. There were no dirty plates, no pots or pans on the cooker. The dishwasher was open a few inches. It was empty. The pine table in the middle of the floor was clean. Apparently no dinner had been eaten, and no breakfast.

"Stone."

I turned. Dehan was in the doorway, staring at me. Her skin looked gray. I felt a sudden, terrible sadness.

She said, "She's in the living room. Brace yourself." She pulled her cell from her pocket and dialed. "Yeah, Detective Dehan, we need a crime scene team and the ME. There's been a homicide . . ."

It was shocking, in the most literal sense of the word. I stood in the doorway, looking at what was left of her, of a human being I had sat with and spoken to, and for a moment the room seemed to rock. There was a ghastly unreality to the scene, and the smell was nauseating. It wasn't the smell of decay, it was the overpowering iron stench of blood. There was a lot of blood.

From what I could see, there was a savage wound to her belly, which was where most of the blood seemed to have come from. Then, postmortem, her head had been severed in what looked like a clean cut. There was very little bleeding from that wound. It was impossible to see anything else.

I felt a hand on my shoulder and turned. Dehan was looking

at me; she was wearing blue latex gloves and held out a pair for me. I took them and pulled them on. "We'd better not go in there till the crime scene team have done their stuff." I pulled the door closed. "The kitchen seems largely undisturbed."

We climbed the stairs and made our way through the bedrooms and the bathroom. The only notable thing was that her bed seemed not to have been slept in. I leaned on the doorjamb while Dehan crossed the room and looked out the window at the street below. "The TV wasn't on," she said. "Unless the killer did the washing up, she didn't have time to cook between Olga Garrido leaving after coffee and her killer arriving. That's a pretty small window of opportunity." She turned to face me. "Are you ever going to tell me what's on your mind?"

I nodded. "Don't forget she was phoned in sick this morning."

"Somebody who didn't want her absence to raise suspicion."

"Two gets you twenty it was the same person who invited her to the reunion. My guess is she was killed either late last night or early this morning. We need to know who invited her—and how. Was it by phone or by email, or post? I'm willing to bet this morning she either got a call asking if she was going, or somebody turned up at the door. The lock was not forced. She let them in. There was no sign of a struggle. The killing was swift and unexpected. She was standing in the living room, facing the door. She took whoever it was in there to talk, and was attacked suddenly, out of the blue, with a very sharp blade. The head was severed postmortem, once she was on the floor. It had hardly rolled at all."

Dehan was nodding as I was talking. "You're right. Last night there would have been people arriving back from work. In the morning, everybody is either delivering their kids to school or gone to work. If it was me, I'd call to make sure she was at home; if she was, ask her to stay. We need to talk, whatever, any excuse." Far off, the sound of sirens stained the bright afternoon with blood. She said, "Motive?"

"Silencing a witness."

She nodded. "Yeah. She sure as hell wasn't shot with a ray gun."

I turned and took the stairs three at a time as the patrol cars rolled up. The CSI team, the ME, and the ambulance were close behind them. I hailed the sergeant, and she came toward me as I was talking.

"I am especially interested in whether the neighbors saw anybody visiting with the victim this morning or yesterday evening. You'll probably find it was this morning. Make, model, and license plates of the car: call my cell the minute you have them. Any of them."

"You got it, Detective."

I collared the ME as he was moving toward the door. "Frank, I have to go. I need to know what weapon was used. Best guess, estimate, intuition. I need to know half an hour ago. Call me or Dehan when you have formed an opinion."

He sighed. "You know I can't..."

"We're not going before the grand jury, Frank! I'm not going to hold you to it, but what I do next depends on your educated guess. Just call me or Dehan when you have an opinion, okay?"

He hesitated.

I said, "Goddamn it, Frank! Might it have been a samurai sword or similar? Just call me and say, 'It might,' or, 'No way!' Can you manage that?"

He scowled at me. "I can manage that. Where are you going?"

"I'll tell you when you call me. Where the hell is Dehan?"

I looked around. She waved to me from my car. We climbed in the Jag. I reversed out, almost taking a patrol car with me, and accelerated up Castle Hill.

SIXTEEN

It took me all of twenty seconds to reach Lacombe Avenue. As we hit the intersection, Dehan said, "Are you going to tell me . . . ?"

I raised a hand. "Don't talk till we get there."

She closed her mouth. I turned left onto Lacombe, drove six hundred yards, and turned left again onto White Plains Road. Another seven hundred yards, then left onto Gildersleeve and left again after just three hundred yards into Pugsley Avenue. I pulled up behind a green Chevy Spark outside Kirkpatrick's house, checked my watch, and looked at Dehan. "That was two and a half minutes. Was that the longest drive of your life?"

"No, Stone, but tonight is going to be the longest night of your life if you don't tell me what the hell is going on and what you are thinking."

I nodded. "I know. I know. I am going to tell you. Just bear with me a moment longer. We have to act fast."

I climbed out of the car and Dehan's phone rang. She got out the other side. "Yeah, Dehan . . . Hi, Frank . . . That's what you want me to tell him? It might well be. That's it? Okay. Thanks." She hung up and squinted at me in the afternoon sun. "Frank. He says to tell you it might well be."

I sighed. "The weapon that killed and decapitated Jane."

"A samurai sword."

"Yeah."

She shrugged, shook her head, and narrowed her eyes. "So what are we doing here? Why aren't we going after Paul?"

"The reunion." Her frown deepened. I pointed at the house. "I want to confirm nobody is here."

She turned and stared at the house, then at me as I pushed through the gate. She looked like she wanted to slap me. I ignored her and said, "Get the back, would you?"

She disappeared around the side of the house. I rang the bell, tried the door, looked through the window, and called his cell phone, all with negative results. His car was gone. Dehan came back around the other side of the house.

"So you proved there is nobody at home. Shall we go get Paul now?"

I nodded. "Yeah. But he won't be there."

She climbed in the car and I got in behind the wheel. She sighed noisily as I closed the door. "He won't be there." She said it in a flat echo of the way I had said it. "Fine. Where will he be, at the reunion?"

"Makes sense to me."

My cell rang. When I answered it, it was the sergeant.

"Detective, we've only canvassed a couple of neighbors so far, but I thought you'd want to know, somebody from the YMCA across the road says he saw a small green hatchback in her drive six a.m. this morning."

I nodded. "Thanks, Sergeant. That's helpful."

I swung the car around and headed at speed up toward Randall Avenue and Paul's gym. It was a short drive, and we made it in just over a minute. I screeched to a halt outside the shopping mall, climbed out, and ran. Dehan was close behind me. The dojo was open, and the first students of the afternoon were just beginning to trickle in, in twos and threes. Dehan smirked and said, "Looks like you were wrong, wiseass."

I shook my head. "No, I'm not."

We entered the school just as a big guy with Marine Corps written all over him stepped out of the office. He had a black belt and bare feet that looked like they could break bricks. He half smiled at us. "Can I help you?"

We showed him our badges. I asked, "Is Paul here?"

He shook his head. "He is away until early next week. I am standing in for him."

Dehan was staring at me. In fact, she was scowling at me. I asked him, "Did he say where he was going?"

"No, sir. He just told me it was a last-minute thing and he would be back Monday or Tuesday."

We thanked him and walked back out into the sunshine.

"Tell me, Stone."

"In a minute. Try his cell. It will tell you it's either switched off or is out of range or something. Try Don and Jasmine. You'll get the same thing. I'm going to call Stuart and May. I'll get the same result too."

"If you know that, why are we doing it . . . ?"

"To prove it, Dehan. To prove it!"

Her cheeks flushed and her eyes went bright. I raised an eyebrow and smiled. She dialed. A voice on my phone told me the number was not available. I opened the car. She was dialing again. I climbed in, and she climbed in the other side. We took off up Rosedale Avenue, back toward the precinct.

Dehan hung up and stuffed her phone in her jacket. "Okay, you were right. Now, are you going to tell me what the hell is going on, or do I just run along at your heel with my tongue hanging out, feeling grateful for whatever crumbs of wisdom you feel like tossing my way?"

"Forgive me."

She looked startled.

I smiled. "I just haven't had a chance to explain, and it *will* take some explaining. I had to check on Don and Paul, and the others, before I could be sure. Now we are going to see the inspector, and then we have a four- or five-hour drive ahead of us. I promise I will explain everything to you as we go." I shrugged. "I meant no disrespect, Carmen, but if you feel like running at my heel and drooling, you know, that could be fun."

"Asshole."

"Funny, that was my mother's pet name for me."

I pulled up outside the station in the shade of a London plane tree, loped across the street, and ran up the stairs to the inspector's office. Dehan was right behind me. I knocked, and he opened the door.

"John, Carmen, come in. What's this about? Sit down."

I shook my head. "There is no time, sir. We need to go to Macomb Mountain and we need to go immediately. We haven't time for the proper formalities, sir, or to clear it with the local sheriff. I'm not even sure what county it is. It might be Essex. Either way, it's a vast area and it's mainly forest, six million acres of the stuff, sir." I shook my head again. "Putting it into the hands of the local sheriff's department will take time, and frankly, the evidence I have is going to sound slim, at best."

He and Dehan were both staring at me like they were worried I had taken leave of my senses. The inspector frowned and said, "If your evidence is slim, why would I be any easier to convince than the sheriff of Essex County, John?"

I looked him straight in the eye. "People are going to die, sir. Possibly tonight. The old UFO group are having a reunion. Jane didn't want to go; she had evidence that might have convicted Danny's killer. She was killed this morning, I suspect to silence her. All the other members of the group are out of town and we can't connect with their cell phones. I have reason to believe they have returned to Macomb Mountain for a reunion. I am pretty sure Don has a cabin up there. You are familiar with the case, and you know I don't go off half-cocked for no reason. I need you to trust me, sir, because if we don't get there in time, those people could die tonight."

He was shaking his head. "Mount Macomb is not within the GOAE of the Forty-Third..."

Dehan cut in and interrupted him with a blatant lie. "Sir, we have worked the last seven days without a break. With your permission, we are taking a couple of days off. This case has got me fascinated by the whole UFO thing, and I need Stone to take me up to Macomb Mountain so I can see where the Danny Brown case started. I hope it will be a quiet couple of days. However, under CPL section 140, we are authorized to act anywhere in the state of New York to prevent a felony, should we be unlucky enough to stumble across one during our time off."

A flash of irritation contracted his face. "Detective Dehan, this is not a game! I cannot authorize..."

"Sir, people are going to die if we don't act..."

He sighed and after a moment nodded. "All right. Take a couple of days off. And for God's sake, if anything happens, call the local sheriff's department! Keep me posted."

"Yes sir, thank you."

I glanced at my watch as we ran down the stairs. It was half past one. We'd get there around five or six. It would still be light.

Dehan was beside me saying, "What's your plan? Where are we going? We can't just drive up to Macomb Mountain and hope we find them. It's a huge area."

We stepped back into the sunshine and started across the blacktop toward the car. "I know, but we are pretty short of options, as everybody who might know where the cabin is is either dead or there right now; and by the looks of it, they either have their cells switched off or, more likely, there's no signal up there." I opened the door and we climbed in. "The way I see it, we have two options." I fired up the engine as she slammed the door, and took off toward the expressway. "Go on Google Earth, find Macomb Mountain, draw a circle around it with an eight-mile circumference, and see what buildings, cabins, holiday resorts—whatever—fall within that area..." I glanced at her. "It won't be much, it is a very remote area. Or ..

." I pointed at the glove compartment in front of her. "Get my copy of *Heaven's Fire* and check the foreword. I am pretty sure at the end it has the date and place where he wrote it. I am not one hundred percent sure, but I have a feeling I saw something . . ."

She had the book and was leafing through the first few pages. She stopped. "Foreword, yadda yadda . . ." She turned the page. "Yadda yadda . . . Here, Elk Lake, 2001. You're a smart man, Stone."

She pulled out the GPS and punched in the coordinates. She spoke as she did it. "We need to stop on the way for toothpaste and toothbrushes, and for lunch. And while we're at it, you can explain to me why the hell it is so important that Donald Kirkpatrick has a damn cabin near Macomb Mountain."

I turned off Story Avenue onto the Bronx River Parkway and started accelerating north. I thought about it for a few minutes, then said, "I'm pretty sure it tells us how Danny was killed."

She took her shades off so she could stare at me better. "I really don't see how, Stone."

"It doesn't tell us who, but it does tell us how. And, here's the thing, Dehan, whoever killed him has started to panic. They were scared that Jane would give us information that would lead us to them. So, we need to be asking ourselves, what did Jane know? What could Jane have told us? What did Jane see, hear, or witness . . . ?"

"Hold on, hold on, hold on . . . Stone, what are you talking about? Jane was killed with a samurai sword."

I glanced at her. The sun made a luminous halo of her hair as the wind whipped it about her head. I said, "So you conclude from this that it must be Paul?"

She made an "isn't that obvious" face and spread her hands. "Who else?"

"Do you know for a fact that Stuart is not an expert in kendo? Or his formidable wife? Do we know for a fact that the person who has summoned them for this reunion in the mountains is someone known to us? How many of the UFO research group became Paul's pupils? Do we have any of this information?"

She sighed. "No."

"Then we must not jump to conclusions, Ritoo Glasshopper. Also, a samurai sword or a similar blade."

"No, Sensei. Yes, Sensei. So you believe that this as-yet-unidentified killer has gathered the group so that he can eliminate everyone who has incriminating evidence. Jane refused to go, so he killed her, and now he is going to kill the rest of them all in one long weekend."

"That seems to me to be the logical conclusion."

"So it has to be somebody who knows that we were skeptical of the UFO explanation and were interested in Paul and Jane's relationship."

"Yes."

She half shouted in exasperation. "That's Paul, Stone!"

I smiled at her and nodded. "You may well be right, Dehan. Either way, I think we are about to find out. Do you think if we just knock on the door they'll put us up?"

"Are you serious?"

"Yeah, why not?"

"How will you explain that you knew they were having the reunion?"

I beamed at her. "Simple. We tell them Jane told us, and see whose eyes pop out of their sockets."

She smiled and looked out the window. Then she laughed. "You're a slippery son of a bitch, Stone. I'd hate to have you as an enemy."

"Funny, that's another thing my mother always used to say to me."

"That she'd hate to have you as an enemy?"

"No, that I was a slippery son of a bitch."

We sped on, ever north, with the big Jaguar engine growling, and the great golden orb of the sun slipping from the midheaven toward afternoon.

SEVENTEEN

We passed Albany and Saratoga Springs, following the I-87. At Glens Falls, we crossed the Hudson for the second time, and at just past Queensbury began steadily to climb. At Lake George, we veered slightly west of north, toward Warrensburg, and suddenly we were ascending into the mountains and into deep forest. On the GPS, it looked like we were close, but the miles kept rolling by and we kept plunging deeper into forest that sprawled, impenetrable, over mountains in every direction.

We passed Schroon Lake and eventually, shortly after four o'clock, we passed a sign for Paradox Lake, which for some reason, at that time, did not seem to bode well. Six miles later we came to an intersection. The I-87 continued north toward Plattsburgh, North Hudson was on the right, and Blue Ridge was on the left. I turned toward Blue Ridge and passed under the freeway. It was like going through some kind of portal into a different world. We were on County Route 84, the forest seemed even denser and closer, the road narrower with more bends, and the only sign of life was the occasional cabin glimpsed through the trees.

The sun was slipping, and though back in the Bronx there would still be several hours of sunlight left, here, among the high peaks and the trees, you had the feeling evening was closing in. We climbed steadily, past Palmer Pond, a large body of black water on our left, and eventually drove through Blue Ridge. Blue Ridge was a town that seemed to consist of two houses, one white and one dark wood, facing each other across a road, surrounded by silent, windowless white barns. We saw no people.

After another two miles or so, we came to a junction. There were no road signs, only a turning to the right. The sun was a couple of inches above the horizon. Everything was motionless and silent. The GPS said it was right, so I turned right and we began to climb again.

Now I realized that what we had seen until now was not dense forest. *This* was dense forest. The road was blacktop—more or less—but it was cracked, pitted, and crumbling at the edges, where roots and undergrowth encroached on the path. This was Man losing the battle against Nature, and, as I drove, I smiled. I looked at Dehan and saw she was smiling too. We were both rooting for nature.

The road wound and twisted, yielding at every turn to the imperative of the trees, and climbing constantly. Finally, after almost ten miles of steady climb, we broke suddenly out of the trees into an esplanade on the edge of a large lake. I pulled up and climbed out. Over on my left, the sun had touched the tops of the trees. Ahead of me, the dark water stretched out for at least a mile, and on my right, half-concealed among tall pines, was a large lodge with a raised veranda. I checked my watch. It was half past five. There was chill air coming off the lake.

Dehan got out of the car. We crossed the esplanade and climbed the steps to push through a door into the reception. The floors, the walls, and the ceiling were all made of wood. The furniture was heavy and solid, and also made of wood, and leather. A fire was burning in a rugged stone hearth. There was a pretty girl behind the reception desk who was smiling at us expectantly.

"Good evening, have you a reservation?"

She said it like she knew we hadn't, because they were all booked up.

"Actually," I said. "We're looking for a friend. He's a writer and he has a cabin up here. He's having a house party with a few guests for a long weekend."

She was very polite. She waited for me to finish and smiled throughout. "Well," she said when I was done, and remembered to smile at Dehan too. "There are not many people around here, even in the summer, so, unless they are new to the area, I am pretty sure I'll know them. What's the name?"

"Kirkpatrick..."

Her face lit up. "Oh, you mean the flying saucer guy! Donald and Jasmine! Sure, we know them. They've been here for years. They don't get out as often these days, but they used to go rambling all over the place, right up to Macomb Mountain, even went as far as Blake Peak one time. Known them since I was a kid."

We all stood smiling at each other. Finally, I said, "So you can tell us where to find them?"

"Well, sure! You're practically there! In fact..." And here she turned to Dehan with a smile that was almost conspiratorial. "You passed it! Ain't it the way? They think they have a great sense of direction, but they ain't!"

Dehan actually gurgled.

The girl said, "You want to go back down the track for like half a mile, and you're going to see a track on your left. Actually, you won't see it. You're probably going to miss it, because it is like just a gap in the trees. You don't want to be looking for it in the dark, I can tell you that! Half a mile, and it's there, where the road bends a bit to your right. It's a dirt track, and you follow that through the woods for two hundred yards, maybe a little more, and you come out to a clearing. And there it is, big old cabin on two floors. You tell them hi from Debbie for me!"

"We'll be sure to do that."

By the time we got back to the Jaguar and started retracing

our steps, the sun had slipped behind the hills. The sky, or what you could see of it, was still blue, but it was a chilly, distant blue, and there were lots of long, dark shadows stretched out across the world.

We found the turnoff where she said it would be. But we only found it because we were looking, and because she'd said it would be there. You only knew you were on a path once you actually turned into it, then it seemed to unfold ahead of you, among the wild, twisting tree trunks, the ferns, and the fallen branches. The canopy overhead was so dense it was almost as dark as night.

Eventually, after two or three hundred yards, a luminous patch of daylight appeared ahead, where the last of the sun's rays lay across a huge log cabin wall, half-engulfed by a wall of giant pines. There were two SUVs and a Focus parked out front. We pulled in next to the Ford and climbed out. The car doors made a muted echo as we slammed them. I looked up at the cabin.

It was a cabin in the way that Windsor Castle is a house. The white pines around it rose to roughly one hundred and thirty feet, towering above the maples, beech, and spruce, but the massive cabin, at the peak of its gabled roof, must have been at least sixty feet high. Broad steps led up to a wooden veranda that stood about three feet off the ground and encircled the building. Beneath it, small windows suggested a basement.

A second floor had a large terrace jutting out over the veranda at the front. Above that, set into the sloping roof, skylights and small windows suggested an attic.

The entire structure was easily the size of four small town houses set in a square and twice as tall. As we climbed the steps, the front door opened, and Donald Kirkpatrick stood staring down at us. He didn't look happy. I smiled, but he didn't smile back.

"Are we to have no respite, Detective Stone?"

"Apparently not, Mr. Kirkpatrick. I thought you might be pleased to see us. We are, after all, taking your UFO theory seriously. May we come in?"

He spread his hands. "I can't very well turn you away, can I?"

It wasn't the most welcoming welcome I had ever received, but it was good enough. I stood back to let Dehan pass, and we entered a very large, very comfortable living room. It was about the size of my house, with a massive stone fireplace, not one but two bearskin rugs thrown in front of it, two leather sofas, and two leather armchairs, each the size of the *Queen Mary*.

Beyond it there was a dining table of similar proportions, with room for at least twelve. It was set with plates, glasses, and bottles of wine. Beside it, a staircase rose to a galleried landing that encircled the room below, giving it a ceiling that must have been twenty or twenty-five feet high. It made it feel more like a cathedral than a house.

Gathered around the fire, the women sitting, the men standing, all holding drinks, were the familiar faces of Paul, Colonel Chad Hait, Stuart and May Brown, and Jasmine Kirkpatrick. Donald said in a loud voice that was as unwelcoming as it was unsubtle, "We have unexpected visitors. Detectives, I believe you know everybody."

The Browns looked curious. The colonel smiled. Paul frowned. He was the one who spoke. "Detectives! Has there been some development? What on Earth are you doing here?"

The door closed behind us and Don advanced toward his guests on long legs. Before we could answer Paul, he said, "And how on Earth did you find us? This place is about as remote as you can get on the East Coast."

I gave it a moment until everybody was looking at us. Then I smiled blandly and said, "Jane told us where it was."

I don't know exactly what kind of reaction I had hoped for, but whatever it was, I didn't get it. The colonel, Stuart, and May gave no reaction at all. Paul looked vaguely embarrassed. Don grunted and muttered, ". . . invited her and she never even answered . . ." and Jasmine seemed not to hear.

She touched her husband's hand and said, "Donald, sweetheart, offer our guests a drink." Then she turned to us and

FIRE FROM HEAVEN | 129

added, "I hope you will join us for dinner. We have more than enough."

I scanned them all again but could find no trace of surprise or shock. I took a couple of steps closer and said, "Mrs. Kirkpatrick, that is very kind of you, but we may not be so welcome when I tell you the reason why we have come."

They all froze. Don scowled.

I glanced at Paul. "I am afraid we have very sad news. Sometime early this morning, Jane Harrison was murdered."

Now there was more of a reaction. May clasped both of her hands to her mouth and stared up at her husband, who looked incredulous. Don seemed to turn gray and sat slowly down on a sofa. The colonel stepped toward him, as though to help. Jasmine, in a strange echo of May's action, clasped her right hand over her mouth while her left clasped her belly. Beside her, Paul swayed. His drink dropped to the floor and smashed, and he reached for the mantelshelf to steady himself.

Don ignored him and looked up at me with hollow eyes. "How . . . ?" he said. "How did they . . . ? Was it . . . ?"

I looked over at Paul. Stuart had stepped forward and was helping him to the other sofa, while May hurried across the room and disappeared through a door into what I guessed was the kitchen. Stuart spoke to the colonel, "Chad, a drink perhaps . . ."

Colonel Hait stared a moment at Paul, then realization dawned and he said, "Oh, Lord! Yes! Yes, of course!" and he hurried to a sideboard beside the fireplace and poured a stiff whiskey, which he then carried to Paul. Paul took it with trembling hands. He took a long pull and shuddered. He looked up at me and asked the same question as Don. "How . . . ? Was it like . . ."

It was Dehan who answered him. "Like what, Paul?"

He frowned at her, sensing her hostility, sensing that something was deeply wrong, but not able yet to put his finger on what. Don exploded, "Goddamn it! Was it like Danny? Was it them? Was it the Visitors? Did they kill her?"

I shook my head. "Oh, no. No, this murder was very human. Very human indeed."

EIGHTEEN

Jasmine, apparently recovered from her shock, stood and crossed the floor to us, gesturing toward the fire, to the sofas and the chairs. Her voice was a little unsteady when she spoke. "Please, Detectives, it has been a long drive, you must be tired and hungry. Please sit, can I get you something to drink? You will stay and eat with us!"

I glanced at Dehan.

She shrugged and almost smiled. "We're not on duty, remember?" To Jasmine, she said, "I'll have a martini, nice and dry, Jasmine, thank you. He'll have an Irish whiskey, large, no ice."

Jasmine went to the sideboard. We approached the fire and Dehan dropped into the chair recently vacated by our hostess. I stood where Paul had been standing, by the fire, and looked at Don. He was watching me, and his expression was resentful.

"Is this part of your commemoration? A kind of tribute to Danny?"

He grunted and looked away. "In a manner of speaking."

Jasmine brought us our drinks, then hurried into the kitchen as May came out with a cloth and a dustpan and brush to clean up Paul's broken glass.

Colonel Hait spoke up, watching me keenly. "It was Jasmine. She had another communication."

Dehan sipped her drink, watching Don as she asked, "Really? When was that?"

"After the conference. After you left."

Hait added, "Right there, in the hall, in front of everybody. It was chilling." He ran his hand over his arm. "It made my hair stand on end."

I frowned. "There is something I don't understand . . ."

May interrupted me. "How *cold* are you people? How frigid and heartless *are you*? You have just told us that Jane has been *murdered*! And you sit there, drinking your cocktails, chatting as though nothing had happened!"

Stuart went to her and knelt by her side, taking her hand in his. "Darling, they are just trying to do their jobs . . ."

She snatched away her hand. "Oh, *leave me alone!*"

She started to sob, and I turned back to Don. "Your whole thesis seems to be that these Visitors, as you call them, are in fact hostile. That the big mistake of mankind is to view them as more advanced than us, benign, with our best interests at heart, when in fact they are no better than human beings, ruthless, heartless predators who view us as nothing more than game."

Colonel Hait was nodding as I spoke.

When I had finished, Don said, "Yes, that is my thesis."

"Yet"—I gestured at them with my hand—"your wife goes into a trance, receives a message about having some kind of a reunion, and here you all are, dancing to the Visitors' tune." I shrugged. "Why? Your enemy tells you to jump and you jump?"

He shook his head. He still looked gray and drawn. "It's not that simple."

"Explain it to me."

"How did she die?"

"It's under investigation. I can't discuss any details with you. She was murdered. Explain to me your relationship with these Visitors, Don."

FIRE FROM HEAVEN | 133

"We don't know anything about them."

Dehan said, "That's your answer? 'We don't know anything about them'!"

Suddenly his face flushed and he was shouting. *"For God's sake! We produced both the Third Reich and Greenpeace! We produced Hitler and Gandhi! Muhammad and Buddha! Surely it is possible that an alien race would be as diverse as we are! We need to connect! Enter into a dialogue! Find out who they are!"*

His bottom lip started to tremble. He looked away and covered his face with his huge hands. The kitchen door opened, and Jasmine came running with short, quick steps. She embraced his head with her arms and pressed his face into her bosom. He clung to her hard and sobbed violently.

There was a generalized sense of embarrassment, and everybody stared at the fire. Except me. I watched Don and Jasmine. "What do you think brought them back now?" I asked.

He took a while to stop crying. Jasmine dried his face with a handkerchief, then kissed his eyes and went back to the kitchen. He shook his head. "Forgive me, Jane's death has come as a shock. All these ghosts seem to be rising up." He looked at me and seemed to take a hold of his emotions. "I can only return, once again, to the simile of the game animals in Africa who are hunted by helicopter. To them, these sudden swoops out of the blue must seem incomprehensible. One day it is a Jeep or a Land Rover that comes, an animal is shot with a tranquilizer, rendered helpless, tagged, and released. Another day an animal that is sick or injured is perhaps cured. And inexplicably, another day, six animals are shot, apparently at random. None of these events seem to make any sense when viewed from the animals' point of view. But from the humans' point of view, it all makes perfect sense, because we know about the game reserves, about the hunting seasons and the hunting licenses, about the poachers and the United Nations and about the preservation of endangered species. The animals don't know it, but they are part of a vast society that both looks after their welfare as species and sanctions their murder as individuals.

We, this primitive human species, are also part of a much vaster society that may well deal with us in the same way."

May spoke suddenly. "Imagine, Detective Dehan, the astonishment of the gamekeepers if one day one of those gazelle suddenly spoke and asked, 'Why are you doing this to us?'"

I looked at Dehan. She had an eyebrow arched while she listened, then said, "Thanks for the insight, honey."

May's face flushed and she looked away.

I smiled to myself and asked Don, "So what did this latest message say?"

He was quiet for a long time. Eventually, he said, "It was very similar to that message, all those years ago. It said that we, the group as a whole, had been chosen as . . . as *messengers*. That certain individuals within the group had specific jobs or functions. It said that we were being given a second chance, that last time we had failed, but that this time we could do it better."

Dehan said, "And it specified that Jane was to be a part of the group?"

He nodded. "Yes, it was quite specific about that."

I smiled and shook my head. "You had failed, all of you, collectively, because Danny didn't go to the glade . . ."

"No! Because I forbade it! And Danny and Jasmine obeyed me!" He glared at me. There was something fanatical in his face. "Remember! They stated that *I* was the rock upon which they would build! Yet when the time came, I lacked faith! I lacked belief!"

"You talk about them as though they were gods . . ."

"Aren't they? Are we not as gods to the animals of the jungle and the savannah?"

I shook my head. "Take it easy, Don. In the first place, animals are not stupid enough to elevate people to the status of gods. For that kind of stupid, you need to be human. In the second place, whatever we may appear to be to a buffalo, what we are is people, plain and simple. We are not insects, and we are not gods."

He waved a hand at me, dismissing what I was saying. "Whatever the case may be! The fact is that they entrusted a mission to me and I failed them, and the result was that Danny died, and now Jane..."

"I already told you that Jane was murdered by a human being. She was not murdered by an alien."

"So you say..."

I narrowed my eyes at him. "So I say? You know something I don't?"

"Of course not, except that they are here..."

"What do you mean, they are here? Here among us. In this room?"

"In a sense, yes."

"Where?"

He sighed. "Stop, Detective. It is not that simple. They are here, believe me."

The kitchen door opened and Jasmine stood for a moment, watching us. "The dinner is ready, if you will sit down."

Donald sat at the head. The rest of us took our places at random around the table, and Jasmine served us with plates of smoked pink salmon garnished only with lemon and parsley. She also brought small baskets of dry toast and water biscuits, while Donald poured chilled glasses of Gewurztraminer.

We ate solemnly and in silence. Occasionally, I would catch Dehan's eye and she would give me a look that asked what the hell was going on. I would give her a smile that told her that was what we were there to find out, and she would sigh and turn back to the salmon, which was in fact very good and very fresh.

In fact, when the colonel eventually broke the silence, it was to look at Don and exclaim, "The salmon is superb..."

"It's fresh. We smoked it ourselves, with wood from the forest..."

He said it not with the pride of a man who has done something unique or admirable, but as though he was revealing some kind of tragedy. I wiped my mouth with my napkin and studied him a moment as he stared down at his plate.

"What is it, Don? What is it you are not telling us? You, out of nearly eight thousand million people, have been chosen to host these alien beings. You are to be the 'rock' upon which they build. And yet..."

He stared at me.

I went on, "And yet, here we are: two dead, two decades gone by, the world in an even worse state than it was during the Cold War, and your 'Visitors,' in order to spread their message, in order to build upon their 'rock,' arrange a meeting in the Adirondacks, with smoked salmon and German wine, and murder a TV production assistant from NBC. It all makes perfect sense. I can see clearly how this will all lead to..." I trailed off and frowned. "Actually, Don, that's a point, what will this all lead to? What is it, exactly, they are building upon the rock that is you?"

He didn't look at me. Jasmine got up and started clearing away the plates.

He shook his head. "I don't know, Stone. And your sarcasm is frankly out of place. You are a guest in my house, you might at least have the courtesy to be respectful of our beliefs."

I nodded. "I am respectful of all beliefs, Don, when they don't lead to homicide. But when people start getting killed, then I become a little less respectful."

"What are you implying," he asked with sudden heat. "That I killed Danny, waited twenty years, and then killed Jane? For what *imaginable* purpose?"

I looked around the table. Everybody still looked embarrassed.

I said, "I don't know. But I guess the same applies to your Visitors. If you, who knew these people, who had close relationships with them, if you have no motive, then what possible motive could a visitor from another solar system have?" I turned and looked at Paul, who was staring fixedly down at the table in front of him. I went on, "The motivation to murder is, in practically every case, the product of a close, intimate relationship, usually sexual. So what motivation would interstellar travelers have to murder Danny and Jane?"

FIRE FROM HEAVEN | 137

Don sighed loudly. "*Again*, Stone? I have already told you! They are hunters, predators..."

"That build churches on the animals they hunt?" I looked at the colonel, who was studying me carefully as I spoke. "That take twenty years between one hunting expedition and the next? Oh, but wait, I am getting confused, was it a religious mission or a hunting expedition? Or do they roll both into one to save time and expense?"

Paul spoke for the first time and his voice was sullen. "You are out of order, Detective."

"Two people have been murdered, Paul, and there are elements of your alien hunter theory that don't add up. Is it a spiritual expedition to build upon the rock of Kirkpatrick, or is it a hunting safari? I just don't buy that it's both, and I don't buy that they came twenty years ago, killed Danny, went away, and came back again to kill Jane. I'm sorry. The theory has too many holes in it."

The kitchen door opened again and Jasmine returned carrying a tray. On it she had two huge meat pies. She brought them to the table on rapid feet, struggling with the weight of the tray. May stood and expostulated, "Let me help you!"

But Jasmine shook her head. "No! No, I can manage!" She placed the tray on the table and gave a small laugh. "You can cut and dish up, if you want to help. Don, we need red wine now."

"I know, goddamn it!" He snarled, "Do I look like an ignorant..." He trailed off, stood, and made his way to the sideboard, where he retrieved four bottles of red wine and brought them to the table, while his wife returned to the kitchen to get potatoes and vegetables. Don distributed the wine. Stuart and the colonel started to pour. As Don sat, Stuart looked at me and said, "Just because we don't understand it, Detective, it doesn't mean it isn't real."

I nodded. "I couldn't agree more, Stuart, but it is equally true that we should not project explanations onto things we don't understand, just to try and get them to make sense. And I fear that is what is going on here. Danny's death was inexplicable. And though your book, Don, makes a very powerful case for the existence of extraterrestrials, it does not, actually, explain Danny's death."

May said, "But neither did the police."

I smiled at her. "But the police left the case open. They didn't close it with an unproven theory."

Don said, "And you think that is what I have done."

I nodded. "I don't think it's what you've done. It is what you have done. And proof of that fact is that, without any of you knowing any details about Jane's murder, you are all attributing her death to the same cause as Danny's."

The kitchen door opened again and Jasmine returned with another tray, bearing large dishes of potatoes and vegetables. She laid it on the table, looked at May, and made a mock cross face. "Ahh! May! You didn't start dishing out pie! Naughty May!"

May covered her face and laughed too. "Oh, Jasmine! I am so sorry!"

I looked up at Jasmine and smiled, and in that moment I caught her staring at Don. She frowned a moment, then her eyes went wide, her face went white, and she screamed hysterically. Next moment, her eyes rolled back in her head and she dropped backward onto the floor, dragging the tray with her, scattering dishes, potatoes, and vegetables in a shattering crash.

NINETEEN

Dehan was on her feet, moving to help Jasmine. Paul was right behind her. Within a second, the colonel followed with Stuart on his heels. May had pushed back her chair and was staggering backward to her feet, screaming. But she was staring at where Jasmine had collapsed on the floor, so I was pretty sure what had scared her was Jasmine's face—not what had scared Jasmine.

Dehan was barking orders at everybody to stand back and give her space. I turned to look at Don. He hadn't moved. He still had his sullen scowl on his face. The only change was that his breathing had grown deeper and faster. He swiveled his eyes to look at me.

I said, "Is this a trance?"

He nodded. I stood and walked over to where Jasmine was lying on the floor trembling. I touched Dehan on the shoulder and said, "Let's get her to the sofa. She may have something to tell us."

We moved in a solemn procession over to the fire. As I laid Jasmine on the sofa, May announced importantly that she was going to run upstairs and get a blanket. Nobody answered her, and after a moment we heard her heels hammering up the wooden stairs and along the landing. Jasmine was now giving the odd tremble, but her breathing was becoming slow and shallow. There was a deep sigh, almost a groan, from the table and Don got to his feet. He came over and stood looking down at his wife.

"Please," he said, "sit. They are about to communicate." He lowered himself into a chair. "Paul, perhaps you would dim the lights."

As Paul went to turn down the lights, May clacked back down the steps carrying a blanket. She strutted purposefully over and covered Jasmine, making sure she was tucked in properly and her feet were covered.

"May . . . ?" It was Don.

She turned to look at him.

He said, "We're waiting. Would you take a seat, please?"

She gave the blanket one last tuck and went to sit next to her husband on the other sofa. Paul joined them. We waited.

Ten minutes passed, with only the sound of the logs crackling and spitting in the hearth. Then there was another sound: the sound of slow, deep breaths, six in total, and then a voice that was not recognizable. It was neither male nor female, but it was deep and resonant, and it came out of Jasmine.

"Jane not here."

I looked at Dehan. She didn't meet my eye. She was staring hard at Jasmine. Jasmine's head flopped on one side, like she was deeply asleep, and a small snore escaped her lips. Then the voice again, with the weird impression that it did not belong to the body it was coming from.

"We have chosen Jane. But Jane not here." Another thirty seconds of silence, then, "Paul."

Paul sat forward. He looked drawn, ashen in the flickering light of the fire. He drew breath to speak, but Don raised a hand. Paul looked at him and he shook his head.

The voice came out of Jasmine again. "We have now chosen Paul. Paul will come to us. At middle of night, at twelve o'clock, he will come to the meeting of three paths, five hundred meters from here. He will know the place. We will give him message for the world."

She seemed to slump again, taking long, slow, deep breaths. Paul was staring at Don. He looked scared. The voice spoke again.

"We have chosen Paul as our messenger. We have chosen Donald as the rock on which we build. There will be other messengers. The world will hear our message. The time has come, now."

She began to tremble again, her legs kicked, and her head thrashed from side to side. I saw May's hands go to her mouth and then Jasmine went still. After a moment, she turned away, toward the back of the sofa, and suddenly, she was just a sleeping woman, and a shadow seemed to lift from the room.

Almost immediately, Paul said, "Don?"

Donald stood and went to the sideboard. He poured himself a brandy and returned to sit by the fire. "What do you want me to say?"

"Are they going to kill me?"

Don shook his head. "How should I know? I don't . . ." He sighed and shook his head a second time. "No. No, I don't think so."

"You don't *think so*?"

A spasm of irritation contracted Don's face. "Danny was killed because he *didn't* go . . ."

I interrupted him. "You don't know that."

He glared at me. "What? What are you talking about? It's obvious!"

"No, it's not." I gave a small, humorless laugh. "That's an inference you've drawn. It's part of the mythology of your group and your readers. But it was never established as a fact. You have no proof of that and, I'll go even further, you haven't even any *evidence*, let alone proof."

May snapped, "Haven't you just seen the evidence with your own eyes? Really, Detective, it is like talking to the wall!"

I ignored her and turned to Paul. "If you are in fear for your life, Paul, don't go. Let's be clear about this. Two people have died: Danny, twenty years ago, and Jane, less than twenty-four hours ago. What connected these two people?" He shook his head. I said, "Two things: this group and you."

He swallowed. "What are you trying to tell me?"

"I'm offering you a reality check, Paul. Please think this through. Danny died in very peculiar circumstances which seemed inexplicable. That led you, amongst others, to conclude that he was killed by aliens. Twenty years later, precisely when we start up the investigation again, the woman you broke up with the night Danny died—because she was in love with Danny—gets murdered. That is one hell of a coincidence. But this time there is no indication of alien activity. This time it is clearly the work of a human being . . ." I paused, giving him time to process what I was saying. "Now *you* are being asked to go out into the middle of the forest, at midnight, to receive a message for humanity from the alleged aliens whom you believe killed Danny. What I am telling you is, be smart and don't go."

Stuart was staring at me like I had just told him Bugs Bunny was behind the murders. "I don't believe what I am hearing. Are you *seriously* suggesting that Jasmine is somehow engineering this? Because that *is* the inevitable conclusion of what you have said."

"At this stage, Stuart, I am not suggesting anything. What I am doing is pointing out that there are several factors connecting the victims with Paul, and I am saying that Paul would be wise to be careful. Can you argue with any of that?"

Don sighed loudly. "Paul, you must be guided by your own lights. There is a lot of common sense in what Detective Stone is saying, but equally I would say that every one of us here tonight knows that Danny was killed because he did *not* go to the rendezvous. I have lived with the guilt of that fact for twenty years and I am not going to make the same mistake again. You must do what you consider to be the right thing. And forgive me for being blunt, but the consequences of that choice will be on you, not on me."

I watched Paul carefully. He sat forward with his elbows on his knees, staring hard at the flames wavering in the fire. Finally, he said, "What time is it?"

Don glanced at his watch. "It's fifteen minutes before nine."

Dehan was watching me, chewing her lip. She was about to speak when the colonel said, "Let me go with you, Paul."

It was Don who answered. "No. None of you seems to understand! The reason Danny was killed was because *he did not stick to the instructions!*"

I cut across him. "Once again, Don, you have absolutely no evidence to support that claim. Now let me make something clear to everybody in this room. We are not in the jurisdiction of the Forty-Third Precinct here, but Detective Dehan and I have the authority to act to prevent a felony in any part of the State of New York. So I am going to tell you exactly what is going to happen. Detective Dehan is going to stay here and keep an eye on everybody in this room. And if you insist on going to this meeting, then I am going to come with you . . ." I looked around at them, one by one, and added, "And be in no doubt that if I have to use lethal force to prevent a homicide, I will do so."

May pulled herself erect. "Now you are threatening to *kill us*?"

Dehan turned on her. "Are you planning to kill somebody, May?"

"*Of course not!*"

"Then we won't need to use lethal force to stop you, will we!"

There was sudden movement from the sofa and Jasmine turned to face us, yawning and rubbing her eyes. She looked around, frowning. "What . . . Donald, darling . . . ?"

He spoke without looking at her. "You had one of your episodes. You had better go up to bed."

She sat up. "I am so sorry. Did I ruin the evening? Did you eat the pies . . . ?"

Donald looked at May. "May, would you mind . . . ?"

"Of course!" She scowled at me and Dehan. "I'll be glad to get away from here. I don't think I can stomach much more of this stench of bacon!" She stomped over to Jasmine and helped her to her feet. "You okay, honey?"

Jasmine smiled at her. "Yes, of course, thank you so much. Just very sleepy."

They proceeded slowly up the stairs and along the galleried landing to the right to what I gathered was the master bedroom. There they went inside and closed the door.

I turned to look at Paul. "I am not enforcing the despotic laws of a police state, Paul. We have very reasonable grounds to believe that a homicide might be committed. Frankly, I don't care if it's committed by aliens or humans." I gestured at him. "You yourself are afraid for your life." I gestured at Don. "Don is worried you might be killed. I don't think there is anybody in this cabin who is not worried you might be killed if you go out there. So you tell me. What do you think my duty is as a New York police officer?"

Colonel Hait was nodding. "There is no question, you are absolutely right, Stone. I cannot argue with that."

Paul sighed. "I hear you. You're right. It's obvious. But still . . ." He looked at me and shrugged. "I would rather go alone."

I shook my head. "Not going to happen. Forget it. Not on my watch."

Don grunted. "We seem to have reached something of an impasse."

Dehan shook her head. "No impasse. It goes down the way we say or it doesn't go down at all."

Stuart snorted and shook his head. "And you say this is not a police state! Yet here you are, ordering us around and threatening us with violence!"

Dehan turned to look at him and for a moment I thought she was going to smack him around the back of the head. Instead, she said, "I don't give a damn about your politics, Stuart. All we want to do is keep your sorry ass from getting killed, and catch your

FIRE FROM HEAVEN | 145

son's murderer. I'm sorry if that runs counter to your damned ideology!"

He had the good grace to look troubled, but before he could answer, the door opened upstairs and May came out on her short, powerful legs and came clacking down the stairs again.

"She is resting peacefully."

She said it like she had pulled off something nobody else could do. She sat next to her husband, with a little waggle of her head, and almost simultaneously Don levered himself to his feet with a grunt and a sigh.

"Well, Paul, the choice is yours. I am exhausted, so I am going to retire for the night. I wish you good luck, whatever you decide."

Paul stood too. "It seems history is repeating itself," he said. "There is no point in my going if you are going to be there wielding a gun, Detective. Who knows, maybe it's for the best. I think I'll retire too."

I stopped him. "Paul, at what time did you come up to the cabin today?"

He stared down at me, momentarily taken aback. "I came up early this morning, with Don and Jasmine. I guess we set out at seven, got here about eleven thirty." He shrugged. "They can confirm that for you."

I nodded. Colonel Hait stood then, muttering, "I'll be turning in too!" And as if on cue, Stuart and May followed suit.

Stuart glanced at me and Dehan and said, sourly, "You certainly make your presence felt, don't you?"

I smiled at him and stood too. In a loud voice, I announced, "Detective Dehan and I will take it in turn to keep watch. We'll sleep on the sofas."

Nobody answered. They all filed up the stairs and made their way to the various bedrooms. The doors closed one by one, and within a few moments the house was silent.

TWENTY

DEHAN AND I SAT STARING AT EACH OTHER ACROSS THE bearskins. There was absolute silence from the upper floor. Dehan stood and came to sit on the rug in front of the fire, where we could talk quietly without being overheard upstairs. She held out her hands to the flames and the rich orange light played on her face. For a moment I regretted that we were there professionally.

"Stone, none of this makes any sense. If Paul is our man, why is Jasmine telling him to go out in the forest in the middle of the night?"

I nodded to show I agreed, then shook my head and shrugged to show I didn't know the answer to her question. I added, unhelpfully, "Somebody is playing a very deep game."

She studied my face a moment. "That trance . . ." She turned back to the fire. "I'm no expert, but that looked pretty real to me."

I agreed. "I've seen people hypnotized before a few times, and when a person goes into deep trance you get a few signs: their pulse slows right down, their breathing becomes very shallow and slow, slightly shorter on the intake than on the exhalation, and the skin goes kind of soft and pasty. They are things that are impossible to fake because they are autonomic responses. She displayed all of them. She was in a trance."

She stared at me again, knitting her brows, shrugged with just one shoulder, and said, "Why do you know that? Normal people don't know that kind of thing, Stone."

"When you're sixty-five million years old, like me, you learn all kinds of useful things."

"Okay, I guess that makes sense." She turned back to the fire. "So why . . . Sorry, so what is inducing these trances in Jasmine? Or *who* is inducing these trances?"

"That is what I hope we are going to find out tonight." After a moment, I added, "It's going to be a long night. I'll take first watch till two, then we'll swap."

She smiled at me and nodded. "Anything, *anything* happens, and you wake me. You got that, Mr. Diplodocus?"

I stood, and she lay on the sofa. I picked up one of the bearskins and laid it over her, hairy side down. She grinned, and I kissed the tip of her nose. "It's Mr. Tyrannosaurus. Get it right."

She chuckled, and within five minutes she was deeply asleep. I grabbed a couple of hefty logs from the basket and stoked up the fire, then I cocked my pistol, helped myself to a generous slice of pie, and poured myself a glass of whiskey. On the bookshelves, I found a volume of O. Henry's short stories and settled myself to wait for whatever was going to happen.

The time passed very slowly. The immensity of the room, the heat from the fire, and the lazy crackle and spit seemed somehow to dilate every minute into an eternity. By eleven o'clock, the lines in the book were beginning to cross and I felt I had sandbags on my eyes. I put down the book, stood, went to the kitchen, and splashed my face with cold water. I tested the kitchen door, found it locked, and slipped the key in my pocket—something, I told myself, I should have done earlier.

I then went back to the cavernous living room, did a couple of circuits, gazing up at the landing, and noticed for the first time the glint of moonlight from the doors onto the terrace.

I climbed the steps and tested the door. It had a dead bolt at the top and another at the bottom. They were both pushed to. I tried them and they were stiff and noisy. Nobody could open them without my hearing them. I peered through the glass. The moon was in its first waning, vast and bright as a spotlight, reflecting off the wood on the terrace, tinting the turquoise sky almost green and making stencils out of the tops of the giant pine trees. Unconsciously, I scanned the sky for UFOs, then sighed and made my way down the stairs again.

I checked Dehan. She was still sleeping. I sipped my drink and looked at my watch. It was eleven thirty.

At eleven fifty, I climbed the stairs again, strolled along the galleried landing listening for sounds of movement, looked out onto the terrace, and saw and heard nothing. At ten past twelve, I went back down the stairs, wondering. I checked on Dehan, checked the front door, then checked the kitchen. All was well, and that worried me, because it shouldn't be.

I returned to stand in front of the fire. Almost simultaneously I felt a chill on my face and heard Don's voice from above.

"Stone..."

He was standing at the railing in his pajamas, watching me. His wife was by his side in a flimsy white dressing gown. She had her eyes closed and she was swaying slightly. He said, "You should come and see this."

He turned and started to walk toward the doors to the terrace. I snapped, "Dehan! Wake up!"

I ran for the stairs, and as I went up them, I realized the cold air was coming from the open door. I swore under my breath and clambered to the landing. Now I could see Don and Jasmine on the terrace with their backs to me, staring at the moonlit forest. I was aware of Dehan below running for the stairs, and the bedroom doors opening behind me. I stepped out.

The night air at that altitude, even in June, was cold, and small clouds of condensation billowed from our mouths. Don turned to me and pointed at the vast black woodland that

FIRE FROM HEAVEN | 149

stretched away under the moonlight. "Look," he said, "look over there."

I approached and looked at Jasmine. Her eyes were still closed. I turned to where Don was pointing. Behind me I could hear Dehan's boots, plus the rustle and shuffle of the others coming through the doors. I said, "I don't see anything."

"Keep watching."

I looked back. Dehan was there, Stuart and May holding on to each other, the colonel, no sign of Paul. I turned to Don. "Where is Paul?"

"Look..."

I leaned over the terrace and stared down. It was possible, for an athlete like Paul, to have climbed down. I cursed myself for not having heard him, and gazed out toward where Don was pointing.

"Where is this meeting of paths, Don? We can't just let him go to his death! Where is he going?"

Jasmine started to tremble. Her breath rasped in her throat and she fell to the floor, shaking as though she were in the throes of an epileptic fit. Don extended his arm, his face drawn and haggard, his eyes staring. "*Look!*"

There, a quarter of a mile away, a vast column of red light beamed down from the empty sky in among the trees.

I heard Dehan breathe, "*Holy shit...!*"

Then we were both running, scrambling down the stairs and across the cavernous room. She got there first and wrenched open the door. Then we were running across the clearing.

The colonel was behind us, shouting, "*Wait! Don is coming! He knows the way!*"

I glanced back. The colonel was waiting for Don, who was running toward us, calling over his shoulder, "*Stuart! May! Come! Come!*" And beyond him was Jasmine's silhouette in the glowing doorway, pushing May, gesturing her to go. Then we were all running behind Don, who was gasping for breath, tall, lanky, and almost comical in his pajamas. He led us deep into the darkness of the forest. None of the brilliant moonlight penetrated the deep canopy of the trees. The only light came from a small flashlight, which he held in his hand and waved erratically across the path as he ran, stumbling over the uneven ground.

It took us maybe four minutes in the dark, following Don's staggering, gasping lead, but we finally came to a clearing, the meeting point of three paths through the woods. It was bathed in the eerie, translucent light of the moon. You could see it was about fifteen feet across and roughly circular. Two more paths, besides the one we were on, wound away from it, one to the right and downhill, the other up and to the left. There was nothing there. No body, no column of red light. I scanned the sky, walking around the clearing, gazing up. There was no trace of the pillar of fire from heaven. Nothing.

"Stone..."

I looked. It was Dehan.

"What diameter would you say that column of light had?"

I thought about it. "Three, four feet?"

I glanced at Hait. He nodded, and we both looked at Dehan.

"That's what I thought. What diameter would you say that has?" She pointed at the center of the clearing, where it was mainly dark moss and grass.

I frowned, trying to make out what she had seen.

She said, "Don't get abducted. I'll be right back," and I heard her boots running back down the path.

Don started after her. "*No! Detective! Where are you going?*"

I said, "Relax. She's gone to get a decent flashlight from the car. Give me yours a minute, will you?"

He handed me his thin pen torch and I got on my knees. There was an area of singed grass which looked roughly circular. It was hard to make out in the poor light, but it seemed to be about four feet across, and everything inside it was burnt. It was not smoldering, and it was not hot to the touch. I looked up at the four faces looking back at me. "Did any of you see smoke at any time since you've been here, rising from this area?"

They all shook their heads. Behind them, I saw the powerful

FIRE FROM HEAVEN | 151

glow of the flashlight I kept in the car. It made a bright halo around their four figures, turning them into smoky, looming silhouettes. Then I heard Dehan's boots, pounding back up the path. She came past them and flooded the clearing with light. I stood. Now it was clear. A perfect four-foot circle burnt into the center of the clearing.

She looked over at me. "So where's Paul?"

I nodded and looked over at Don. He, the colonel, May, and Stuart were all gazing up at the sky. I said, "Colonel, take these people back to the cabin and make sure Jasmine is okay, will you? We'll join you in a minute." I handed him the small flashlight.

He looked startled for a moment, then took it and nodded. "Yeah, sure..."

Don, Stuart, and May started back down the path. I said quietly, "Colonel?"

He stopped. "Yes, Stone?"

"Are you armed?"

"Why, yes. I have a license, obviously..."

"I have no doubt. Just keep your weapon with you at all times, will you?"

He looked uncomfortable, then nodded again. "Yes, of course." He turned and hurried to catch up with the others.

I watched the small, dancing speck of light recede, thinking of the powerful glow of Dehan's flashlight as she had approached, thinking of the powerful beam of light we had seen from the terrace, perfectly straight, not fanning, not spreading, not a cone, more like a giant laser.

Dehan brought me back from my thoughts. "Is he dead?"

"There are two possibilities. He has either done a runner, or he's dead."

She shook her head. She looked exasperated. "But he is the only person with a motive! What the hell was that thing? It just beamed down out of the sky! There was nothing there and suddenly, zap!"

Nearby an owl hooted and a small predator rustled in the

underbrush. I nodded at Dehan and started pacing around the clearing, chewing my lip and going over the sequence of events as I remembered them. "I came out of the kitchen. I felt the cool air from the terrace. I had not felt it twenty seconds before when I went in. Don called me up, said I had to see something. I ran up. The terrace door was open and he and Jasmine were out, looking over this way, like they knew. I stepped out. He was telling me to look over where we were about to see the lights. He had obviously called everybody else because they all came out at the same time. Jasmine had her eyes closed throughout the whole thing. Then she started trembling. Next thing, she made that weird noise in her throat and fell. In that moment the light appeared . . . and we ran." I shook my head. "There just wasn't time, in the twenty seconds that I was in the kitchen, for all that to happen. I tested the bolts. They were stiff and squeaky. I didn't open them because I didn't want to wake you up."

"So, in the time it took you to go into the kitchen and . . . do what?"

"Check the door."

"Nothing else?"

"Nothing."

"Paul came out of his room, slid back the two dead bolts without making a noise, opened the door, clambered over the terrace, and shimmied down to the clearing, while also somehow alerting Don and Jasmine, the colonel, and Stuart and May."

"It is not physically possible. It can't be done."

"And when we get here there is no sign of him. So how did they know? How did they know to come out of their rooms?"

"We have been played," I said. "We have been played, Dehan. We have been played good."

She shook her head. "I don't get it."

"Paul never left his room."

"Shit! We need to get back!"

"No, he won't be there."

"Where, then?"

FIRE FROM HEAVEN | 153

I stared at her for a long moment, then I stared up at the few, distant, icy stars I could make out through the glow of the moon. "I have a feeling I know," I said. "But you may find it hard to believe. Come with me..."

And I turned and headed up the path, winding like a narrow tunnel ever deeper into the impenetrable shadows of the forest.

TWENTY-ONE

We returned to the cabin about half an hour later, by way of the trunk of the Jag, from which I collected my laptop. We found them all seated about the fireplace drinking hot cocoa laced with whiskey. Stuart opened the door to us and let us in.

"Did you find anything?"

I shook my head and went to stand in front of the fire. Jasmine got to her feet and took hold of Dehan's hands. "May I make you and Detective Stone some hot drink? Everybody's having some. It is very comforting. This has all been such a shock."

Dehan smiled. "Thank you, that would be great. Stone?" I glanced at her and nodded. Jasmine disappeared into the kitchen, and I turned to look at Don. He was staring into the flames. He looked exhausted, wrecked. I examined May and Stuart, and the colonel. They all looked like Don, drawn, scared, depressed. There was nothing remarkable about any of them.

Don said suddenly, "I believe he will be returned to us. I believe that. This was not like Danny. *Not* like Danny! He didn't disobey. He was not mutilated, incinerated . . ."

Stuart nodded. "I agree with you. It was just the singeing from the beam on the grass. He was clearly simply beamed aboard to receive whatever instruction he needs for the mission he has ahead of him..."

I stared at him for a moment, frowning.

Dehan shook her head in a gesture of disbelief, and for a moment I thought I could see her father in her, as she had described him to me. She was half smiling, half exasperated. "Clearly? Seriously? That is *clearly* what happened? Would you mind telling me exactly what evidence you have that makes that clear to you? Because, I have to tell you, I didn't find a shred out there. All I found was a circle of burnt grass."

Stuart sighed and groaned and rolled his eyes. "Detective! What is it going to *take* for you to open your eyes and *see* what is going on here? You cannot take an isolated incident on its own. It is *cumulative*! *Everything is connected!*"

She nodded and offered him a lopsided smile on the left side of her face, where it was more sarcastic than ironic. "Oh, sure! Cumulative. Like the cumulative evidence that proves the sun orbits around the Earth." She pointed at him. "Is that what you think you have done? Opened your eyes? This, what you all are doing right here, this is an act of faith! Worse! It's *superstition*! You, under the guidance of a man who claims to be a scientist, are constructing an entire belief system on an unfounded assumption! You have not got a single piece of objective proof! Not one! Nothing! You're saying, 'We don't know how Danny was killed, therefore he *must* have been killed by aliens.' And after that, everything and anything that you can't explain gets explained the same way. Now, you even know that they operate training programs for their missions. Based on what? *On a patch of burned grass!*"

I watched her and felt a warm glow of admiration.

May shook her head and muttered, "You couldn't begin to understand."

The kitchen door opened and Jasmine came out with two mugs of cocoa. She took them to the sideboard and smiled at Dehan. "Cognac or whiskey, Detective?"

I watched Dehan turn, and for a moment she seemed to move in slow motion. She reached behind her head and took hold of her long, black hair, tied it in a knot as she spoke, and as she did so, my mind raced and I understood everything. The whole thing became suddenly crystal clear. I seemed to snap out of a dream and heard Dehan say, "Whiskey, please, Jasmine."

I watched Jasmine lace them generously and hand them to us, first to me, without making eye contact, and then to Dehan, with another smile. After that, she left us and went to clear the table. Dehan raised the mug to sip from it. I pointed at the mug and said, "Be careful, you might burn your lips."

She stared at me with the mug halfway to her mouth with a slightly incredulous smile. "What are you now, my mother?"

"Do me a favor, would you, Dehan? Just go up and have a look at Paul's room. See if he packed a bag. See if his pajamas are there, or if the clothes he was wearing are there. Let's see what he had on when he disappeared. You can leave your cocoa. It'll still be there when you get back."

I took it from her hands and placed it on the sideboard along with mine. As Dehan ran up the stairs, I turned to Kirkpatrick.

"I wonder, Don, if you could deliberately induce one of Jasmine's trances."

He looked slightly surprised. "What are you suggesting? That I somehow engineer these experiences? That is absurd!"

I shook my head. "No, that's not it at all. I am trying to keep an open mind. I was thinking about what Detective Dehan said about the complete absence of proof. If these beings—assuming that they exist at all—but if what they are trying to do is communicate with us, then perhaps we could take the initiative and use Jasmine not just as a receiver, but as a *transceiver*, and communicate to them the predicament they have put us in, and see if we can get some concrete proof of their existence, maybe even solve the mystery of the murders." I looked around at the four astonished faces and laughed. "I've been trying to tell you from the start that I have an open mind. All I want is a

FIRE FROM HEAVEN | 157

reasonable standard of proof. If this can get it for us, we should try."

Kirkpatrick stared past me at the dining area. I followed his gaze. Jasmine was standing by the table with a pile of plates in her hands, watching us. After a moment she nodded, then turned and made her way back to the kitchen. Kirkpatrick looked back at me. His eyes were penetrating. "What do you have in mind?"

I shrugged, spread my hands. "We simply create the conditions for the trance. We kill the lights, let her lie out on the sofa, and you speak to her. Tell her to relax, to open her mind to the Visitors, to call on them. You know the kind of stuff. I don't need to tell you. I'm sure you've attended a few sessions of hypnotic regression in your time. I guess it would be pretty much the same thing."

He nodded. "Yes, it is possible, we could do that."

I went on. "Then, when we have contact, Detective Dehan will put the questions to them and explain our situation. Let's see how they respond."

Stuart had been frowning at me. Now he turned to Kirkpatrick. "I have to say I am surprised, Donald, but it does seem to make sense. It is at least worth a try."

Kirkpatrick nodded. "Yes, I agree." He turned to me. "What if they instruct you, as they did Paul, to go to the clearing?"

"Then I'll go."

"Very well."

He stood and went into the kitchen. Dehan came out of Paul's room and crossed the length of the galleried landing to the doors out to the terrace. I watched her unbolt them and step out. A moment later, Kirkpatrick and his wife came out of the kitchen and he led her to the sofa, where she lay down and got comfortable. Upstairs, Dehan came in from the terrace and I went up to meet her. We came down together and I explained to her what I had arranged with Don.

"You want to take care of the questions?"

She looked surprised. "Me? Why?"

I smiled. "I liked the way you expressed it earlier. You put my own thoughts into words very nicely."

She raised an eyebrow at me. "Jeez, boss, thanks. It's going to look great on my résumé. Next thing, I'll get headhunted by the Alien Negotiation team at Langley."

I laughed, and as we approached the group, I said, "What were you doing on the terrace?"

Again, she looked surprised. "I was trying to see how he got down. I can't figure it. His clothes are all in his room. He must have been wearing pajamas. It's crazy."

I nodded. "Okay." Dehan sat close to Jasmine's head, where she could talk to her when the time came, and I addressed the group. "All right, we are going to see if we can get some answers to our questions. There is a lot that you guys take for granted, but we haven't got that luxury. We need facts and we need proof, so that is what we are going to try and get. Detective Dehan will conduct the session once Don has induced a trance in Jasmine. Meanwhile, I am going to record it on my laptop. Just try to ignore me, and forget I am here. Detective Dehan is the person you need to be focusing on."

I went and switched off the lamps from the main console. The only light now was from the fire, and from the moonlight filtering in through the windows. I set up the laptop on the dining table and sat behind it. When I was ready, I said, "Dehan . . . ?"

She turned to look at me and held up her thumb, and I knew that from where they were, I was all but invisible behind the dim glow of the screen. I said, "Whenever you are ready, Don."

A moment later, I heard a soft cough, and then the gentle murmur of his deep voice as he took her through a relaxation routine that told me he was no stranger to hypnosis.

"As you are listening to my voice, allow your mind to move inside you, and notice how you become aware of all those feelings that are telling you that you are becoming deeply, deeply relaxed . . . all the way down. That's right . . . *all* the way down . . ."

Even without listening to the words, the rhythm was

soporific. The deep, burnished light from the fire flickered over the group, causing long shadows to waver and dance across the room. Jasmine lay in a deep pool of darkness on the sofa, invisible to me where I sat. His voice droned on.

". . . you know that the power of . . . your unconscious . . . now takes you deeper than you have ever gone before . . . into realms of . . . your unconscious . . . so deep and so high that you can reach up with your mind, among the stars, and open . . . your unconscious . . . to the minds of visitors from other worlds . . ."

I had set my chair back so that it was easy to stand without making a noise. Now I stood and made my way up the stairs, listening carefully to Don's voice, alert to any change that would tell me he had noticed my absence. There was no such change. His voice continued, repeating over and over, ". . . your unconscious . . ." suggesting images of space and stars and sleep.

I reached the galleried landing and moved quickly along to the doors to the terrace, which Dehan had left open for me, as we had arranged. I stepped out and walked quickly to the side. There I pulled myself over and, with some difficulty, clambered down and dropped to the ground below, with only a few scratches and grazes. Then I ran to the back of the house and scrambled under the veranda to the small window we had opened on our way back from the clearing in the forest. The flashlight was where we had left it. I shone it through the window into a very large cellar crammed with everything from old furniture and cardboard boxes to sacks of logs, a washing machine, a big spin dryer and a freezer, a large trolley, and everything else you would expect to find in the basement of a mountain cabin.

I dropped the flashlight onto an old, dusty chair, dragged myself through, and lowered myself onto that same chair. Once down, I took the flashlight and stood in the middle of the floor, playing the light over the walls and into the corners, making a more detailed inspection, and one by one I began to find all the things I had expected to find when it had dawned on me that the party had been at a cabin in the mountains.

All but one.

Then I turned the flashlight to the washing machine, the dryer . . . and there was the big chest freezer. I approached it, and with a vague sense of nausea, I opened it. And it was there, as I had thought it would be. Or rather, they were there: the head, a ghastly white with blue lips, and his eyes mercifully closed. Beside it, his feet, and beside his feet, his genitals. All neatly contained in plastic bags.

I closed the lid. The torso, then, must also be where I had imagined. That was the other part of the puzzle which had dropped into place. But before I could check, behind me I heard the door open, and Don's voice spoke in a harsh rasp.

"Don't move, Stone, or I swear I will blow Detective Dehan's head clean off her shoulders."

TWENTY-TWO

I TURNED. THERE WAS A FLIGHT OF WOODEN STEPS UP to a door. That door now stood open onto the kitchen, and in the opening I could see the silhouettes of Dehan and, just behind her, Don. He seemed to have a hold of the back of her collar in his left fist, and in his right I could make out what seemed to be a pump-action shotgun.

"Where are the others? They are not in on this, are they?"

"That doesn't concern you."

I played the light over them. I saw Dehan wince and cover her eyes. Don did the same. I shifted it a little and said, "I haven't much to lose, Don. You are going to kill us anyway, aren't you?"

Dehan said, "I'm sorry, Stone. I started questioning Jasmine. He got up, and when he came back, he had a shotgun . . ."

He shook her savagely and snarled, "Shut up!"

I said quietly, "Hurt her and I'll kill you where you stand, Kirkpatrick."

He snorted. It may have been a laugh. "Do as you're told and nobody need get hurt."

I gestured with my head at the freezer. "Like Paul? Like Jane?"

"This could have been simple and painless, Stone. You chose to make it complicated—and painful."

"The law, Don, the law made it complicated and painful. The law that says it's not okay to go around murdering people, however justified you may feel in doing so."

"Don't lecture me. I am too old and I have seen too much of the world to take lectures from the likes of you. Now put down your gun."

I gave a single bark of a laugh. I pulled my gun from my holster and showed it to him. "I put this down and I sign Detective Dehan's death warrant along with my own." I shook my head. "No, we are going to have to talk about this." I frowned. "I am curious. What have you done with the others?" I turned and pointed at the freezer. "You knocked him out with sleeping tablets, the way you tried to do with us, with the cocoa. But I don't believe you knocked out the whole party that way. No, I don't think that was your plan at all. I think you actually wanted witnesses..."

I stepped toward him. He backed up and shook Dehan again. "I'm warning you, Stone! I will kill her!"

I shook my head. "No, you won't. You know as well as I do that the moment she is dead, the balance of power shifts in my favor. You will put off killing Detective Dehan to the last possible moment. And that is why I am going to hold on to this weapon." I moved toward the steps and began to climb. He backed up. I went on talking. "I made a lot of mistakes in this case to begin with. One of my first was to believe that your wife was as much your victim as Danny was. Then I shifted and thought that maybe you were your wife's victim." I stopped at the top of the stairs and stared into Dehan's face. She was frowning, confused. Then I looked past her at Donald Kirkpatrick. "Both made sense, yet neither made perfect sense. Then it dawned on me, only tonight, that you were partners. That you were acting together."

I turned and walked out of the kitchen into the vast living room. There, Stuart, May, and Colonel Hait sat together on the sofa, looking frightened and confused. Jasmine stood by the fire. She held a .38 revolver in both hands, trained on the colonel.

May watched me walk in and said, "What the *hell* is going on?"

I gave her a lopsided smile. "You asking the bacon, May? I couldn't begin to understand, remember?"

Stuart looked at me resentfully. "This is not the time for scoring points, Detective Stone!"

I gave my head a little twist to the side and made a "tsk!" sound. "If not now, then when, Stuart?" I looked at the colonel. There was a question in my eyes: Had he relinquished his weapon? I knew he read me, and he seemed to nod. The .38 was his. I sat in the armchair with my gun on my lap and looked at them all. Don and Dehan were close behind me.

Don shoved Dehan toward the sofa and said, "Sit down!" Then he turned to me. "Okay, Stone, now you hand over your gun. If you don't, we start shooting. We start with May, then Stuart, then the colonel, and finally your partner."

I made a face like I wasn't really convinced. "I don't know, Don. I grant you, you have a strong hand, but it sounds to me like you're not thinking very clearly. Let me explain the situation to you. Here you have two senior detectives from the Forty-Third Precinct of the New York Police Department, who have gone for a long weekend up to the Adirondacks while in the middle of an investigation, and they have gone to the very spot where the case they are investigating started . . ." I smiled, gave a small laugh, and shook my head. "Clearly this is no coincidence, and it is merely a device to get around jurisdictional red tape. So you must realize that our chief is aware of where we are, and what we are doing here. And in fact, he will be expecting to hear from us tomorrow morning."

Jasmine was staring at me with no expression on her face at all. Don glanced at her, then back at me. He swallowed. I went on.

"Now, maybe, if you are *real* smart, you might get away with killing all these witnesses and pretending it was the aliens who did it. Everybody will know you are lying, but if there is no evidence, you *might* just get away with it." I laughed. "But a sofa full of bullet holes and soaked in blood? I don't think so. We are at an impasse, Don. You both know it."

He snarled, "You think we are incapable of taking them outside one by one and executing them?"

"Oh, I think you are very capable of that. But the moment you pick somebody, I am going to put a bullet through your head." I looked over at Jasmine. The only change to her expression was that her face had gone tight; other than that, there was nothing. I said to her, "How about that, Jasmine? Life without Don. The rest of your life in a women's prison, knowing that Don was dead. That appeal to you?"

Her eyes flicked over at him and I saw fear.

He snapped, "Don't listen to him! We can do this!"

I said, "I'm curious about something. Just indulge me for a moment, and then we can get back to how we solve this impasse . . ."

He frowned, smelling a way out. "What do you mean, 'solve'?"

I laughed. "Come on, Don! We are all grown-ups here. I am sure we can find a solution where everybody wins." I played a hunch and gave Jasmine a sly look. "You know what I'm talking about, don't you, Jasmine?"

Don said, "Some kind of deal . . . ?"

"We'll come to that. Just indulge me, I'm curious. How this whole thing started, way back in '98. Back then, you were no part of this, were you?" I looked at Jasmine. "You were just a mail-order bride, right? Young—what were you, twenty-five, twenty-six, excited, a little out of your depth, swept off your feet by a husband who, though he was a lot older than you, was fun, exciting, even a bit glamorous, right? You must have been blown away by the whole thing."

I waited. She didn't answer. She just stared at her husband. There was terror in her eyes. I pushed on.

"And, you know what I'm curious about? Were you interested in UFOs back in the Philippines? Or was that something you just got involved in through your husband? Either way, it must have been pretty cool to have the cabin for the weekends, and come out to the mountains, and all of Don's friends who'd come along too..."

I let the words trail away. She was staring at Don real hard. She was willing him to do something. All of her attention was on him, and I could have shot her right then without her ever realizing it, but the risk of Don shooting Dehan in retaliation was too high.

"Trouble is," I said, "however much we have, we always want something we don't have, isn't that right? And you had it all, Jasmine, but, like the desperado, you wanted something you couldn't have. You wanted Danny, didn't you?"

She shook her head. "No, not true."

I laughed quietly. "Come on, Jasmine, the game is over. It's time to admit the truth. You saw him, and right away you fell in love, but you were totally dependent on Donald, for everything, from your resident's permit to your food and the roof over your head. Not to mention the way of life to which you were rapidly becoming accustomed. So what to do?" I wagged a finger at her. "And I bet that was when your mind went back, almost without thinking, to the things you had seen as a kid. Where are you from in the Philippines, Jasmine? Let me guess. Western Samar? Maybe Sorsogon...?"

She nodded. "Sorsogon..."

"And you had often seen the trances of the Mangkukulam, you knew how it looked and how convincing it could be. And you were right. It fooled everybody. Especially as nobody expected it from such a shy, obedient young girl like you." I turned to Don. "It fooled almost everybody. It didn't fool you, though, did it, Don? You were really in love with your new bride. You doted on her. It really surprised me when Paul told me that, because now you treat her like dirt. But back then, you doted on her. You doted on her so much that you were aware of her every desire, and you noticed the tiniest nuances and changes in those desires. And however hard she tried to hide it, you noticed when she started to turn cold on you, and started to hunger for Danny. You saw the concealed looks, the gazes, the blushes, the smiles . . . those million and one tiny giveaways that tell you somebody's feelings have changed. You noticed." I shook my head. "I'm guessing you would have been willing to ignore it, if she only hadn't acted on it. Am I right?"

He curled his lip. "If you think you are going to get me to admit anything . . ."

"Come on! What difference does it make? I'm a cop! I'm curious! But by the end of tonight, you're going to have as much on me and Dehan as we have on you." I turned my smile on Jasmine. It wasn't a nice smile. "If you had just been willing to love him from a distance, it would probably all have blown over. But you are not the type, are you? You are the type who, when you want something, you go after it, in your own shy, secret way, but you go after it. That, after all, is why you're here in the States, right? Because you will go the extra nine yards.

"You wanted Danny, but you were never alone with him. You were always with Don. Plus, in the beginning, I bet Danny didn't respond to your secret come-ons, did he? He loved and respected Don, and he would never have betrayed him. But bit by bit, he started to become fascinated. Because you were not quite like any woman he had ever known before. And you began to notice that he liked you.

"So that night, that awful, fateful night in June, 1998, you pretended to go into a trance, you thrashed around as you had seen the Mangkukulam do, and then you spoke your silly, childish lines, that you and Danny were the chosen ones, and, to keep him happy and make him feel important, you borrowed a line from the Bible and told Don he was the rock on which they would build. And after everything they had just witnessed on Don's specially adapted equipment, they were all taken in . . ." I turned to Don. "Except you. You saw right through it, and you saw right through it not just because you could read Jasmine like a book, but because you knew that everything they had all just witnessed on your specially adapted equipment was a crock of horseshit. You knew there were no aliens out there trying to make contact. You knew it was all a scam. I don't know if you borrowed the technology from Jane, or if she was in on it with you, but all your group saw that night on Macomb Mountain was special effects, wasn't it?"

He nodded. "Yes. I knew they were there. I still know they are there. But I was sick of waiting. I had been promising so much to my group, to Jasmine, but they would not show themselves to me. And I could see Jasmine losing interest, becoming ever more drawn in, like everybody else, by Danny's magnetism and charisma. They were all drifting away from me. Jane had no idea, but I picked her brain over a few weeks and put something together. For a little while that night I tasted success, and Danny was in awe of *me* for a change."

"And then Jasmine had her trance, and you knew. You knew that she had decided to sleep with him, and once she did, it would be over. Your love affair, your marriage, your dreams, the group—everything would be over. So you forbade them to go, and in forbidding it, in trying to terrify them into obedience, you remembered the cattle mutilation cases, and the Brazilian case in Guarapiranga, amongst others, and in that moment, the idea was born in your mind. *You* wouldn't kill him, the aliens would."

May was shaking her head, staring from me to Don and back again. "No! *No!* Donald? It's not true! Donald? How? How? We have been over this a thousand times!"

"How?" I said. "With Jane's help, that's how."

TWENTY-THREE

They all stared at me in disbelief. May said, "*Jane?*"

I shrugged. "She didn't know she was helping, but it was all those conversations on special effects that gave him the idea. And I confess it was very clever. It only dawned on me what he had done when I realized that he had a cabin up here in the mountains. Because, when you think about it, even though the whole spectacle was mesmerizing, there was only one small part of it that was actually impossible. And it was that small detail that made the *whole thing* seem impossible."

The colonel was frowning, and Stuart was squinting at me like I'd just told him two and two made plum donut. "What are you *talking about?*"

I smiled. "It gets a little confusing, I know. And it was that simple fact that helped consolidate this as one of the classic cases in UFO mythology. Because, you see, Jasmine was not alone in being infatuated with Danny. Jane also had a big crush on him. And that night, she became jealous because she realized, with her feminine intuition, that Jasmine was coming on to him, in her own quiet, subtle way, and that he was liking it. So she made her play and tried to seduce him. The net result was that she got nowhere with Danny, but made Paul very mad, and where there was supposed to be a party at the cabin on Saturday night, instead, Paul and Jane's bad feelings spread throughout the company and everybody ended up going home early.

"And that confused me to start with because I had assumed that everybody was going home from your place in the Bronx. But they weren't, they were going home from here, and Danny stayed. What did you do, Don? You sent Jasmine to bed. She's so obedient she would do anything you told her, right? So you sent her to bed and, what? Did you shoot him? Stab him?"

May let out a ghastly, inhuman wail. "*Oh, no! Dear God, no, please!*"

I stared at her and wondered for a moment at a mind that could accept her son's death at the hands of extraterrestrials, but the thought of his being killed by another man was intolerable. I turned back to Don. He sighed.

"I stabbed him with a kitchen knife. Poor boy. He was very surprised." He turned to look at May and Stuart. "I'm sorry. It was very quick. He hardly suffered at all. I stabbed him from behind, directly into the heart. Left the knife in until the heart had stopped beating, so there was practically no bleeding."

The horror on Stuart's face, and on May's, was beyond words. They stared at him, and not just the horror of their son's death was written large in their eyes, but also the twenty years of betrayed trust, the twenty years of calling him a friend while all the time he had been their son's executioner, all the while he had held the memory of their son's death in his mind. I didn't want to go on. I didn't want to subject them to any more, but I had no choice.

"You took him down to the basement, as you did with Paul tonight."

"Tonight was more difficult because Jasmine had to do it alone, while we were out at the clearing. She had to use a trolley. You probably saw it in the cellar. But that night I did it myself. I cut off the head and the feet and . . ." He hesitated and scowled at

May and Stuart, who had gone sickly white. "Well, I was angry!" he said. "Trying to fuck *my wife!*" His face flushed with rage, then it slowly subsided. "I kept the bits in the freezer and put his body in the furnace, on a sheet of metal from an old oil drum. It gets damn hot in there. You need a lot of heat to get through the winters up here. It drops to well below freezing, and you have snow for months on end . . ." He might have been giving one of his lectures, or narrating a travelogue. "When he was reduced to ash, with a few bones, I gathered him up and put it all in a cooler in the back of my car, and drove back to the Bronx."

Colonel Hait was staring at him, transfixed somewhere between horror and fascination. "But how? For twenty years, the murder has been unsolved *because it was impossible!* Even Detective Ochoa ended up accepting it must have been some kind of nonhuman agency!"

I smiled and nodded. "Believe me, Detective Dehan and I were scratching our heads and beginning to wonder if this was a genuine X-File. But actually, it was really simple." I spread my hands. "If it had just been the lights over the park, that's simple, right? A remote-controlled chopper, or helium balloons with some kind of directional fan to drive it around, a few lights and a few lasers bought from an electronics store. With a little advice from Jane—albeit unwitting advice—something like that was easy to put together."

Don was nodding. "It was a helium balloon with a directional fan, much like a zeppelin. I had been planning to use it for a sighting up here in the fall . . ."

I continued, "Even the mutilation and the incineration were not impossible to explain, as you've seen, but what made it seem impossible, what acted as a catalyst to make the whole thing seem impossible, was the absence of footprints or tracks. Any explanation you came up with fell apart when you tried to explain how the body got there. And *that* was what fell into place when I realized that there was a cabin out here. Suddenly the house had to have a furnace, for the long winters—a furnace capable of producing the necessary temperatures to incinerate a body. And when you have the furnace, you are no longer carrying a hundred-and-sixty-pound body, you are carrying much less weight; and if you have a furnace for the snowy winters, well, you're also going to have snowshoes, right? Snowshoes, possibly adapted with a bit of sheepskin, or wool, would leave no recognizable tracks across the mud. And then everything else fell into place."

I smiled at Dehan as she closed her eyes and slapped her forehead with the heel of her hand. "Son of a *bitch*!"

"And the little spectacle tonight? Paul was given some sleeping tablets ground up in his drink. That's why he retired early." I looked from Don to Jasmine. "Which one of you two lovely people did it?"

Jasmine blinked.

"Oh, it was you, was it? You slipped into his room and stabbed him. Then we were lured out to the terrace, and that 'beam' you were so certain had come down and teleported him up to be instructed for his mission, had not come down at all. It had shot up. It was a couple of hundred dollars' worth of lasers, of the sort you might use at a rock concert, stuck to a board in a small clearing thirty yards from the meeting of the three paths. It was triggered, I have no doubt, by a remote control concealed in her dressing gown pocket. She had her fit, collapsed in a trance, and triggered the light display. We went running from the house, led by Don to the exact spot where we were to find the singed circle he had made earlier with a blowtorch."

Dehan was shaking her head, staring at Jasmine. "But why? Why would you collude in all this? He murdered the man you loved!"

I laughed out loud, and Dehan stared at me in genuine shock. I spread my hands. "It was the best thing that ever happened to her! Don found himself being driven, almost in spite of himself, to write up the case of his charismatic friend and colleague, fallen in his passionate pursuit of the truth. Interest in that kind of story in the media in those years was at an all-time high. The chance was too good to pass up. He wrote the book and published it and, if before he was comfortably well off, suddenly his book had sold over a million copies, and twenty years later it is still selling and the case has become a UFO classic. Overnight, Mr. and Mrs. Kirkpatrick had become millionaires." I looked Don in the face. "Of course it destroyed you as a person. You became this . . ." I gestured at him. "This bitter, twisted residue of a human being. But you . . ." I turned to Jasmine. "You'd never had it so good!"

Dehan was nodding. "But when we reopened the case, Jane and Paul suddenly became a liability. And when you saw that we were getting too close and we wouldn't buy the ET explanation, you decided Jane and Paul had to go."

I nodded. "Exactly." I turned to Jasmine. "My money is on you. I think it was your idea. You are deep and dark, and I think you suggested it to Don. Let's not just kill them, let's use it as the basis for a second book that will sell even more than the first one. A commemorative reunion in the mountains, where Jane, Paul, and Danny's parents are all mysteriously killed in exactly the same way as Danny, and you, Colonel, would have the honor of being the survivor, the credible witness who saw the whole thing happen, the beams of light from heaven, the trances. You would provide the alibi for the killers."

Stuart stared at Don, his eyes bulging. "You were going to kill *us*?"

Don scowled at the floor. "Don't you want to join your precious son?" He turned to me. "Enough of this. What's this deal you are suggesting?"

I waved my gun at the colonel, May, and Stuart. "We kill them, Dehan and I provide you with the alibi, and we get fifty percent of the proceeds from the book."

Hait's jaw dropped. "*What?*"

May screamed and covered her mouth with both hands, staring at me with eyes wide with fear.

Stuart was shaking his head frantically. "No! Don, no! We won't talk! Listen to me! *For God's sake!*"

Jasmine spoke. She looked at Don. Her eyes were hard and pitiless. "I don't want to share."

Don snarled, "If they don't call into the precinct tomorrow, people will come looking for them. We *need* a credible witness! Without a witness we have nothing!"

Suddenly Hait's face was flushed red. "*I don't believe you people! Have you gone insane! This is murder you're talking about!*"

Don went scarlet and screamed at him, "*Shut up! Shut up! Shut up!*"

And then Jasmine was screaming, "*I don't want to share! We don't share! We kill them! Kill them!*" Then she swung her gun arm around, pointed at my head, and screamed, "*No share!*"

She squeezed the trigger. There was a violent flash and a huge explosion. Jasmine was lifted off her feet and hurled back against the fireplace with a big, ugly, red-black hole in her chest, while the slug from her gun tore through the back of my chair. Dehan was on her feet. She had her left arm wrapped around Don's gun arm; she had aimed the shotgun at Jasmine and pulled the trigger with her right. I gaped and scrambled to my feet as she smashed her left elbow back into Don's jaw. He staggered away and fell to the floor, leaving the gun in Dehan's hand.

Next thing, Stuart had jumped up and hurled himself at Don. I shouted, "*Stuart! No!*"

But he ignored me and fell on Don with his hand clasped around his neck, screaming, "*I am going to kill you, you son of a bitch!*"

I grabbed him by the scruff of his neck and dragged him off. Then Don was scrambling to his feet and running. Dehan bellowed, "*Freeze! Stop!*"

But he ignored her, wrenched open the door, and ran. Stuart pulled free from my grasp and went after him. I shouted, "*Stuart! For God's sake! You damned idiot!*" And as I shouted, I was running. Dehan was just ahead of me. We burst through the door and out into the night. The moon was declining toward the west, but by its light we saw Don hurtle across the clearing, with Stuart close behind, and disappear among the trees, headed in the direction of the lake. We went after them. As we ran, Dehan indicated she would go right and I should go straight, and before I knew it, she had peeled off among the trees and disappeared.

I swore violently under my breath. It is easy to get lost in a forest in broad daylight. In the middle of the night, it is almost impossible not to. Thankfully, the trees were less dense here and some moonlight did filter through, plus we were on a slope that I guessed ran down to the lake. I slowed from a mad dash to a steady run, trying to listen for sounds ahead. I could clearly make out the noise of heavy bodies crashing through the undergrowth, but whether it was Don, Stuart, or Dehan was impossible to tell. And the peculiar acoustics of the forest made it equally impossible to pinpoint the location.

I had figured that if the track we were on led to the lake, it was a fair bet there was a boat at the end of the track. If Don made it to the boat and managed to row to the other side of the lake, it would be impossible for us to catch him. But a more immediate worry was that, though Stuart was in the grip of a wild rage right now, he was not a killer. Don was, and I had no doubt Don would kill Stuart to get away. And all of that added up to the fact that I had to catch Don, and I had to catch him before Stuart did.

The trees started to thin and suddenly I had broken out onto a moonlit beach. Globules of amber light warped and glimmered on the black water. Ten paces away, the black hulk of a rowboat loomed on the shore. A man stood motionless beside it. It was impossible to tell if he was facing the water or facing me. I had my back to the mass of the trees and I wondered if he could see me. I stepped silently forward a few paces.

Then there was a sound, a movement. A shadow rose up out of the black form of the boat. It swung an object, possibly an oar, and struck the motionless figure on the back. There was a grunt and a thud, but by then I was shouting, "*Freeze! Drop it! Freeze!*"

I ran forward and came around the hulk of the boat. I could see them grappling now in the sand. Stuart was screaming, making shrill, incoherent noises, gripping Don's throat. Don was pounding his face with his fists, but it seemed to have no effect. I holstered my weapon and moved forward to grab Stuart's collar, but suddenly Don was kicking sand and scrambling to his feet, running for the lake, and Stuart was up and going after him. Don's plan was clear, and I shouted, "*Stuart! No!*"

I had no shot. The risk of hitting Stuart was too high. I swore for the second time and made to run. But in that moment there was a streak across the sand. A black form hurled itself at Stuart's legs and he went down flat on his face.

I ran to him, and as I grabbed his wrists and knelt on his back, Dehan snarled, "Cuff him!" And she was off.

Don's tall, willowy form was wading into the water. For a moment, he looked like some strange, ancient creature of the woods, tall, thin, and angular, waving his arms like branches as he went deeper into the dark liquid, with the pale moon touching his skin and the small waves around him.

The moment didn't last. Dehan crashed through the water, holding her weapon in both hands, shouting at him to stop. He turned to face her, almost waist-deep now. Perhaps she thought he was going to surrender. Perhaps that and the dark, and her innate reluctance to shoot an unarmed man, all conspired against her in that moment. But he lunged, took the gun from her hands, and in the next moment, he had dragged her under the water.

It may have been a fraction of a moment. It seemed to be an eternity of stillness and silence while he stood, with his back arched and Dehan gone beneath the black, enveloping water of the lake. I was not aware, in that moment, of what I was doing. I heard a voice screaming Dehan's name. I felt the splash of cold against my body. I saw an automatic weapon in front of me in the darkness, in the strange moonlight. I saw it kick once, twice, three, four—seven times, and then it was just clicking. Don's dead body lay on the surface of the lake, staring blindly up at the universe, at the empty stars that in the end had given him nothing. I screamed again, "*Dehan!*"

I dropped the gun and reached beneath the small waves with frantic hands, searching for her clothes or her hair, or anything to grab hold of. And then the lake exploded, and Dehan erupted from the inky depths like a whale, spraying foam and hair in all directions, screaming, "*Son of a bitch! Where are you, you mother...!*"

Her fist and elbows were going like a windmill on speed. I reached for her with both hands. "Dehan! Dehan, it's me, Stone, stop! Stop!"

"Don! Where is he? *Where is he?*"

"Dead. He's dead. I've got you. Come here..."

She came to me and I held her tight, and we stood and trembled together, waist-deep in the cold black lake, under the moon, with Don's dead form drifting slowly toward the shore.

EPILOGUE

WE EVENTUALLY PULLED DON'S BODY ASHORE, dragged him onto the sand, and covered him with a tarpaulin from the boat. I then uncuffed Stuart, who was sobbing and shivering like a small child, and we had walked back up the track to the cabin. There we had found that the colonel had telephoned the sheriff's department and that the sheriff was on his way with several deputies.

By the time he, the ME, and the CSI team had arrived, and he and his deputies finished taking detailed statements from everybody, the sun was already rising over the giant pines in the east, and the birds were getting busy singing and doing whatever it is birds do in the early morning. A warm copper mist was rising off the grass, and the sky seemed to stretch and yawn as it turned from dark to bright blue and the moon finally sank down in the west.

The sheriff promised to forward his report to the Forty-Third and asked us, as a courtesy, next time we wanted to shoot somebody in his county, to let him know beforehand. We had promised we would and driven away.

At the bottom of Elk Lake Road, we had come to the intersection with County Route 84. There I had turned left, headed back toward the I-87, New York City, and the Bronx. Along the way we passed once again through Blue Ridge, and shortly after that we had come to a small cottage on the left, set back among the trees, and there must have been at least a dozen ancient, half-rusted signs posted outside it. Everything from "County Route 87," to arrows pointing to campsites, gas stations, and nature reserves. There was something beautiful about the woods and the cottage, and even about the signs that seemed to belong to an older, simpler world.

But the sign that really caught my eye was bigger than the rest. It was a long, wooden arrow pointing back the way we'd come. It was painted brown with white letters in the style of the old west. It said, "Adirondack Buffalo," and under that it said, "Bison meat."

I pulled over to the side of the road. Dehan looked at me without much interest and said, "What are you doing?"

"I'm calling the inspector."

She gave a single, upward nod. While I dialed, she said, "That was pretty neat, Stone, about the snowshoes and the furnace... Simple, when you know..."

The phone rang on the other end. I shrugged. "It just made sense."

"So who killed Jane?"

"I figure it was Jasmine. Five-minute drive early in the morning. Jane would let her in. She had no real quarrel with her. Her pretext was to convince her to come to the reunion. Jane insists she won't, and Jasmine kills her."

"What about the whole samurai sword thing?"

"Eskrima, the ancient Philippine art of fighting with blades. We will never know for sure, but my guess is she had some training."

"Huh! And what the hell is a Mangku...?"

"A Mangkukulam. A practitioner of Philippine voodoo." The phone stopped ringing and I got the inspector's voicemail. I said, "Hi, Inspector, it's Stone here. We got lucky and managed to

FIRE FROM HEAVEN | 179

wrap up the case. The Essex County Sheriff's Department will be sending over their report. We're on our way back, but we seem to have got a little lost. Cells just don't seem to work up here, sir, no signal at all. But as soon as I can, I'll call you. If I can't, expect to see us no later than, say . . . Tuesday."

Dehan burst out laughing. I swung the Jag around and headed back into the mountains. I had seen a sign earlier for Aunt Polly's B&B. I figured with a name like that, it couldn't be bad. And nearby was The Cellar, on Long Lake, where they were bound to do bison steak and good artisan beers. I began to smile and looked at Dehan. The sun was shining, she had the wind in her hair, and she was grinning behind her shades. She looked like a million bucks wrapped for Christmas, and I felt like the luckiest man alive.

Don't miss TO KILL UPON A KISS. The riveting sequel in the Dead Cold Mystery series.

Scan the QR code below to purchase TO KILL UPON A KISS.

Or go to: righthouse.com/to-kill-upon-a-kiss

NOTE: flip to the very end to read an exclusive sneak peak...

DON'T MISS ANYTHING!

If you want to stay up to date on all new releases in this series, with this author, or with any of our new deals, you can do so by joining our newsletters below.

In addition, you will immediately gain access to our entire *Right House VIP Library*, which includes many riveting Mystery and Thriller novels for your enjoyment!

righthouse.com/email

(Easy to unsubscribe. No spam. Ever.)

ALSO BY BLAKE BANNER

Up to date books can be found at:
www.righthouse.com/blake-banner

ROGUE THRILLERS
Gates of Hell (Book 1)
Hell's Fury (Book 2)

ALEX MASON THRILLERS
Odin (Book 1)
Ice Cold Spy (Book 2)
Mason's Law (Book 3)
Assets and Liabilities (Book 4)
Russian Roulette (Book 5)
Executive Order (Book 6)
Dead Man Talking (Book 7)
All The King's Men (Book 8)
Flashpoint (Book 9)
Brotherhood of the Goat (Book 10)
Dead Hot (Book 11)
Blood on Megiddo (Book 12)
Son of Hell (Book 13)

HARRY BAUER THRILLER SERIES
Dead of Night (Book 1)
Dying Breath (Book 2)
The Einstaat Brief (Book 3)
Quantum Kill (Book 4)
Immortal Hate (Book 5)
The Silent Blade (Book 6)
LA: Wild Justice (Book 7)

Breath of Hell (Book 8)
Invisible Evil (Book 9)
The Shadow of Ukupacha (Book 10)
Sweet Razor Cut (Book 11)
Blood of the Innocent (Book 12)
Blood on Balthazar (Book 13)
Simple Kill (Book 14)
Riding The Devil (Book 15)
The Unavenged (Book 16)
The Devil's Vengeance (Book 17)
Bloody Retribution (Book 18)
Rogue Kill (Book 19)
Blood for Blood (Book 20)

DEAD COLD MYSTERY SERIES
An Ace and a Pair (Book 1)
Two Bare Arms (Book 2)
Garden of the Damned (Book 3)
Let Us Prey (Book 4)
The Sins of the Father (Book 5)
Strange and Sinister Path (Book 6)
The Heart to Kill (Book 7)
Unnatural Murder (Book 8)
Fire from Heaven (Book 9)
To Kill Upon A Kiss (Book 10)
Murder Most Scottish (Book 11)
The Butcher of Whitechapel (Book 12)
Little Dead Riding Hood (Book 13)
Trick or Treat (Book 14)
Blood Into Wine (Book 15)
Jack In The Box (Book 16)
The Fall Moon (Book 17)
Blood In Babylon (Book 18)
Death In Dexter (Book 19)
Mustang Sally (Book 20)

A Christmas Killing (Book 21)
Mommy's Little Killer (Book 22)
Bleed Out (Book 23)
Dead and Buried (Book 24)
In Hot Blood (Book 25)
Fallen Angels (Book 26)
Knife Edge (Book 27)
Along Came A Spider (Book 28)
Cold Blood (Book 29)
Curtain Call (Book 30)

THE OMEGA SERIES
Dawn of the Hunter (Book 1)
Double Edged Blade (Book 2)
The Storm (Book 3)
The Hand of War (Book 4)
A Harvest of Blood (Book 5)
To Rule in Hell (Book 6)
Kill: One (Book 7)
Powder Burn (Book 8)
Kill: Two (Book 9)
Unleashed (Book 10)
The Omicron Kill (Book 11)
9mm Justice (Book 12)
Kill: Four (Book 13)
Death In Freedom (Book 14)
Endgame (Book 15)

ABOUT US

Right House is an independent publisher created by authors for readers. We specialize in Action, Thriller, Mystery, and Crime novels.

If you enjoyed this novel, then there is a good chance you will like what else we have to offer! Please stay up to date by using any of the links below.

Join our mailing lists to stay up to date -->
righthouse.com/email
Visit our website --> righthouse.com
Contact us --> contact@righthouse.com

facebook.com/righthousebooks
x.com/righthousebooks
instagram.com/righthousebooks

EXCLUSIVE SNEAK PEAK OF...

TO KILL UPON A KISS

CHAPTER 1

"Do you know how many times I have stood at this breakfast bar watching you cook bacon and eggs, wanting to tell you how much I love you when you cook bacon and eggs?"

It was seven o'clock in the morning and the smell of bacon and coffee was strong and rich on the air. She didn't look at me, but I could tell she was smiling. She said, "Yup."

"How many?"

She wielded the spatula with dazzling skill and slipped two eggs onto each plate as though it was easy. "I'm not going to tell you because then we'll get all mushy and we'll have to go upstairs and shower again. Put these on the table."

I carried the plates to the table with a self-satisfied saunter and a slightly foolish grin on my face. I sat, and as I reached out to pour the coffee, I felt her breath and her lips on my ear as she whispered in a husky growl, "Why d'you think I did it, dumbass?"

We were rescued from having to rush back to the shower by the jangling of my cell phone.

"Stone," I croaked. She grinned and sat.

"Good morning, John, it's John here."

I frowned, then my head cleared. "Oh, Inspector, good morning."

"Good morning. I'm sorry to call so early. I'm probably interrupting your breakfast. Look, I have a letter here, maybe nothing, but you never know, do you . . . ?"

I waited. He waited. I said, "No, Inspector, I guess you don't. What is the letter about?"

"The Westchester Angel."

I groped my way through the fog of coffee, bacon, and Dehan toward a dim glimmer of recollection. "Jane Doe, spring 2016, they found her body by the Westchester Creek. Raped and strangled."

Dehan was chewing, watching me with narrowed eyes, nodding slowly. Inspector Newman continued. "Probably raped, that's the one. Indeed. The writer claims to have information relevant to the case, and as the case has gone cold, I thought perhaps you would like to talk to him."

"Sure, of course. Give me his number. We'll give him a call and drop by . . ."

"Well, here's the thing. I've made an appointment for you to go and see him, this morning at nine, hence the early call."

"An appointment . . ."

I frowned. Dehan frowned in sympathy, sipping black coffee from her white cup.

"Yes, he's at Rikers, serving five years for possession of cocaine. His name is Wayne Harris. You can collect the file on your way. It's waiting on your desk."

"Thank you, sir . . ."

"See me when you get back. Let me know what he says."

"Yes, sir, we'll do that, as soon as we get back."

"Good. Nice talking to you. Enjoy your breakfast, John. And, uh, catch you later!"

I could hear the smile in his voice. I said, "Yes, sir, catch you later too . . ." But he'd already hung up.

It is a pretty roundabout route to Rikers Island from Morris Park, involving Randalls Island, the Robert F. Kennedy Bridge twice over water, and the Francis R. Buono Memorial Bridge just once. On the way we collected the file on the Westchester Angel case and Dehan read out loud while I drove. She had the window down, and the late May sun bathed her face as she raised her voice above the battering air and the growl of the Jaguar.

"Exactly a year ago, almost to the day. Monday the sixteenth of May, 2016, a body was found on an area of wasteland that runs for about half a mile along the west bank of the Westchester Creek. It was spotted by an employee at the quarry opposite the FedEx depot, who called 911."

I frowned. "Where was the body?"

She studied the file a minute, holding the pages between her fingers like a cigarette, to stop them flapping. After a moment she said, "Yeah. Zerega Avenue?" She glanced at me and I nodded. "You got the FedEx depot, the Golden Mango warehouse, and the quarry. There's a big patch of trees and rocks right on the river. She was down there." She carried on reading aloud. "Time of death was impossible to establish, as always. She'd been lying out in the open by the side of the river and lividity was advanced, though decay was still only in the initial stages. It was estimated that death occurred at some time between Saturday afternoon, when the guys from the quarry would likely have spotted her if she had been there, and the small hours of Sunday night to Monday morning."

We were crossing the first portion of the Robert F. Kennedy Bridge onto Randalls Island. I asked, "Cause of death was strangulation, right?"

She nodded, chewing her lip. "Mm-hm. She had some bruising to the face, especially the mouth, consistent with having been slapped hard or punched. ME suggested whoever hit her was big, or at least had large hands. Her wrists had been bound very tight with a silk handkerchief . . ." She looked at the photos and made a face. "But not like you'd expect. It was more like the old-fashioned cuffs. Like"—she held out her wrists to demonstrate—"he tied one wrist tight, then left some slack and tied the other wrist, so there was some play. Like he wanted her hands to have a certain amount of freedom." She shrugged. "Cause of death was strangulation. There was extensive bruising to the neck, the windpipe had been severely crushed, and the pattern of the bruises suggested that was done with the thumbs. No prints were recovered, so the killer probably used gloves."

My frown deepened as we passed over the sports fields and began to cross the water toward Astoria Park. "How was she lying?"

"Facedown, half in the water. Postmortem found that she'd had sex, so she may have been raped, premortem, perimortem, or postmortem. The semen was too decayed to provide a DNA profile."

I grunted. "Odd."

"What is?" Before I could answer, she said, "If she was raped Saturday night, say eight or nine o'clock, she could have been lying there about forty-eight hours, half in the water. The semen could well have decayed in that time."

I nodded, but I didn't say anything.

We crossed the long bridge over almost a mile of water, and she read me the last part of the file, about why Detective Ibanez had not been able to close the case. The victim had had no purse, no driver's license, no ID on her. There were no witnesses and her DNA and prints had got no hits on CODIS or IAFIS. All they had was the fact that she was Hispanic, in her early to midtwenties, and had a rather beautiful, expensive crucifix around her neck, inscribed with the name "Angela" on the back. Her clothes—a white blouse and a gray skirt—were good quality but modest and demure. The two latter facts had earned her the name the Angel of Westchester Creek in the more sensationalist press.

Three quarters of an hour later we were sitting in an interview room looking at the photos of the crime scene while we waited for Wayne Harris to be brought in. "I need to see it," I said.

Dehan nodded. "There are a couple of things I don't get . . ."

I agreed, but before I could say so there was a loud clang and the steel door rolled back. Two uniformed guards led in a tall man in an orange jumpsuit. He had the look and build of a quarterback: about six foot five, and I estimated his weight at about two hundred and thirty or forty pounds of solid muscle. He had a face that looked hard and solid too, with short hair, a square, raw concrete jaw, and a small, thin, cruel mouth that seemed permanently fixed in a thin, cruel smile. He had small, pale blue eyes, which he used now to observe Dehan as though he was calculating her size, weight, and intelligence.

The guards sat him in the chair opposite us and cuffed him to a metal ring on the table. One of them, a beefy black guy with humorous eyes, said, "If he gives you any trouble, you jess shout. We're right outside."

I thanked him, and they strolled out and clanged the door shut behind them. Wayne didn't look at me. He kept his eyes on Dehan. When he spoke, it was like sandpaper being dragged over twenty years' accumulated deposits of hardened nicotine in his throat.

"It's sure nice to talk to somebody who ain't a con. You ain't a con, are you, Detective?"

I said, "I'm Detective Stone, this is Detective Dehan. We're from the cold-cases unit at the Forty-Third Precinct. I was told you had some information for us."

He kept staring at Dehan, smiling, then slowly shifted his gaze to look at me. "Well, that all depends, Detective Stone of the Forty-Third Precinct. See, we are in the age of the Information Revolution. That may be something you don't fully appreciate, on account of your age. But Detective Dehan here, I figure she is closer to my age. Am I right, Detective Dehan? I figure maybe you will have a better understanding of what I am talking about. Information is where it's at. It's the name of the game."

Dehan raised an eyebrow at him that could have sliced the balls off a brass monkey.

I smiled and said, "If you're looking to sell information, Wayne, however old I may be, you need to talk to me. I run the cold-cases unit."

He still didn't look at me. He frowned and smiled simultaneously at Dehan and said, "Ouch! Male chauvinism strikes again. The white male still running the show, huh?"

I stood. "When you're ready to talk to me, Wayne, call the precinct. Right now you've got time to waste; we haven't."

Dehan stood.

Wayne sighed. "Take it easy, man! Take some time out from being you, we'd all be grateful." He grinned. "You feel me? Know what I'm sayin'?"

I waited, watching him. "Have you got something for me?"

"Yeah, man! Siddown, I got something for you."

I sat. Dehan went and stood in the corner, behind me, leaning against the wall with her arms crossed. I smiled to myself. She knew he wanted to play games with her, so she'd gone where she could observe him without distracting him. Now he was looking for her with his eyes.

I said, "You know something about the Westchester Creek murder in May 2016?"

He looked pained and gestured toward Dehan. "C'mon, man. She don't have to go away."

I leaned forward. "Okay, Wayne, this is your second warning. There won't be another. I think you're bored and you want to play games, and you know exactly squat about the Westchester Angel. Now you had better start talking as soon as I draw breath or we are out of here and you will not see us again. Start talking now."

"Okay! Okay! Okay . . . man! Heavy or what?"

I stood.

"I'm talking already! I was there! I saw the whole damn thing go down. I watched it! All right?"

I sat. "No. You're lying."

"I ain't lying! I was there, man."

"Prove it. I'm out of patience, Wayne. You need to keep me here and I am walking..."

"I was near the bushes, lyin' there just minding my own business, watchin' the stars, smokin' some weed, you know? And I hear this noise, like people strugglin', and I look over and I see this dude comin' down from the road, where there is a gate in the fence, and he has a chick with him and he is pushing her in front of him."

"Why didn't she scream?"

He started to laugh. "Well, I didn't ask her, Detective Stone Cold. I didn't think I was invited to that particular party. You feel me? But I *think*—and you know it was kind of hard to see in that light, at that time of night—I think she had a gag in her mouth."

"What time was this?"

"Now, let me see, you're gettin' very particular and maybe my memory needs refreshing..."

I stood. "You're full of shit, Wayne."

"Ten or ten thirty Saturday night! Man! Don't you *ever* let up? All I'm askin' for is a little two-way reciprocity, dude."

"Give me something I don't know, then we'll talk about reciprocity."

"I'm settin' the scene. Chill. So he takes her down, where it's kinda like a beach. You been there?"

I nodded.

"It kinda levels off toward the water, and there's grass and it's a bit soft there, so you can lay down. And he throws her down on her back, he pushes up her skirt, and he rides that baby. Man! And he's tellin' her to hold him. Weirdest fuckin' thing I ever saw. 'Cause she's got her hands tied, right? And he's kissin' her like crazy, and when he comes up for air he's sayin', like, 'Hold me, bitch! Hold me!' And she can't say nothin' back because he's in this kind of frenzy, kissin' her and stranglin' her at the same time. When he's done, he pulls up his pants, and he starts to drag her toward the water. I guess he's figurin' on dumpin' her in the river. But just at that very moment . . ." He leaned back in his chair and started to wheeze with laughter. "You would not believe it, man! I mean, what are the chances, right? That is the very moment a Harbor Patrol boat chooses to just cruise on by. You should have seen that guy hightail it out of there. Man . . . he was like a dog with a jalapeno pepper up his ass!"

I thought about it for a moment. "Did you get a good look at him?"

He made an exaggerated grimace, sucked his teeth, and drew a deep breath. "Well now, Detective Stone Cold, here's how I figure it. I have given you enough that you *know* I was there. And you *know* I saw what I saw. Now, I have smoked a lot of dope in my time, and I have snorted a lot of coke, and you know how it goes. That shit can affect a man's memory. Not so much that he forgets things for*ever*! You feel me? But just so much that he needs a bit of *stimulation* for his memory. Am I wrong?"

I sighed. "What do you want?"

He wheezed his unpleasant laugh again. "Man . . . *man*! I have spent my whole life askin' myself that, and I *still* don't know. What do you want, Wayne? The sweet lips of a beautiful woman, the taste of a *fine* cigar that has been rolled on the thigh of a *Cubana* . . ." He leaned forward across the table. "A cup of real coffee, man, so many things. Where do I begin to tell you, man, what I want when I have lost my freedom?"

I sighed, like I was really bored, put my hands on the table, and went to stand. "Well, Wayne, what can I tell you? If you won't tell me what you want, then we can't make a deal."

"Okay, okay, okay . . . You get me out of here, man. I can't be in here. This place is full of dudes who *need* to be in here. You know what I'm sayin'? Like, they *want* to be in here. It's like some weird shit, unconscious drive to be in prison and, like, *controlled*! But I ain't like that. I need to be outside. I am a free spirit. You get what I'm sayin' to you?"

I shook my head. "I can't get you out of jail, Wayne. You were found guilty of being in possession of cocaine. You have to do your time. It's the law."

"*You* can't get me out of jail, but you know a man who can. Am I wrong? You can make it happen, Detective Stone Cold. Don't tell me you can't, because I know you can."

I shook my head again and stood. "To do that I would need a lot more than a description of the crime scene, Wayne. You haven't told me anything I didn't already know . . ."

He smiled and interrupted me. "But I told you enough that *you* know I was there and I saw it go down. Think about it, Detective Stone Cold. Think about it and we are gonna talk again."

"Goodbye, Wayne."

"Goodbye, Detective Stone Cold." He leered at Dehan. "I'll catch *you* down the road, Detective Dehan."

Ten minutes later we climbed into my Jaguar—an original right-hand-drive, burgundy 1964 Mark II, with spoke wheels—and rolled down the windows to let in the sun. Dehan stared at me and I stared out the windshield.

She said, "I think he's full of crap."

I nodded several times, then turned the key in the ignition and fired up the big engine. As we pulled out and started the long drive across the dark water, I said, "I want to have a look at the place. I also want to have a look at what the press said about the murder, what details we released to them. We should talk to Ibanez too."

She raised her aviators up like a medieval visor and squinted at me, frowning. "He said something that caught your attention. He said something you want to check against what the press reported, because you think only somebody at the scene could have known it."

I laughed. "You asking or telling?"

"Both. I'm asking but I know I'm right. What was it? What did he say?"

"You remember I said something was curious, and you thought I meant the decay of the semen?"

FIRE FROM HEAVEN | 199

"Uh-huh."

"I didn't. What struck me as curious was the fact that he had crushed her windpipe with his thumbs. But she was lying facedown."

She made a face and nodded. "So he was trying to move her."

"Right. The report you read made no mention of that. So I want to know if the papers or the TV did. Because if they didn't. . ."

She was nodding. "He did. He said the killer tried to move the body into the river, then ran when the Harbor Patrol came by."

"Yup. So we need to pull up the reporting from the time. Because if he was there, either he saw who did it, or . . ."

I looked at her and she said, "Or he did it."

CHAPTER 2

WE FOUND A SPACE TO PARK OUTSIDE THE GOLDEN Mango Supermarket on Havemeyer Avenue and walked the short distance to Zerega, which runs along beside the creek. There is a stretch between the quarry and the FedEx depot, about a hundred and forty yards or so, where the road borders the riverbank, separated only by an ugly fence made of steel tubing and wire mesh, about eight feet high. It serves little purpose, other than to make a place that should have been beautiful even uglier than it had already become: it was both easy to scale and easy to cut through.

Dehan touched my arm and pointed. "There's a gate over there. It's open."

I followed her over and examined the gate. There were scratches that suggested it had once been secured by a chain and a padlock, but both were long gone. Dehan pushed the gate farther open and we squeezed through into a miniature jungle of tall grasses, weeds, ferns, bushes, maples, and oak trees. I stood a moment, absorbing the scene. Dehan pushed farther in, following what might have once been a beaten path, taking big, arching steps over weeds and nettles with her long legs. She had the file with her.

I called out, "I think the body was down there." She turned to look at me and I pointed to the right. "There should be an inlet down there, with a rocky beach, and a grassy lip, like a small mound."

She nodded and started picking her way to the right a bit. I followed and we came out onto a sloping bank of mixed rocks, sand, and moss that descended steeply for about eight or nine feet to a small knoll, roughly oval, about twelve or fifteen feet long and six or seven feet across at its widest point. It was surrounded on three sides by tall grass and shrubs, but on the far side it sloped gradually down to a rocky inlet in the river. Dehan pulled out the pictures of the crime scene. "That's it, there," she said, and we scrambled down to the knoll.

She stood a moment examining the pictures again while I peered over her shoulder. She pointed ahead, to the edge of the grassy lip. "Her body was over there, facedown, with her right arm pinned underneath her and her left arm kind of flung out toward the river." She shook her head. "I can't make out any drag marks . . ."

I turned and looked back, in the opposite direction. "He probably rolled her. That's why her arm is pinned. If you drag a body you have to do it from the feet, otherwise they are almost impossible to move. If Wayne was telling the truth, he would have been over there, in those bushes."

I pointed up at a patch of undergrowth about thirty feet away. Dehan turned, looked where I was pointing, and nodded. She said, "So right now I am asking myself, if . . . *if* Wayne has knowledge of the crime scene and the position of the body, that was not made available to the media, what's to stop us from promoting him to prime suspect?"

I shrugged with my eyebrows. "I was wondering the same thing."

She echoed my eyebrow-shrug with her shoulders. "The only thing I can think of is that, if he was the killer, he would have to be really stupid, seriously stupid, to draw attention to the fact that he was here at the time of the murder. And he struck me as a lot of things, but stupid wasn't one of them."

I scratched my chin, still staring at the area where Wayne had said he'd been lying, getting stoned and looking at the night sky. He would have had a perfect view of the events. I sighed. "Agreed. He's not stupid, at least not in the sense of having a low IQ."

I clambered up to the spot, lay down, and looked up at the sky. I called down to her, "What did Ibanez make of it?"

Dehan was quiet for a bit, leafing through the file. "She didn't really come to any firm conclusions, but she speculated that the most likely explanation was that Angela, if that was her name, was a prostitute and was killed by her pimp or a client."

I winced, sat up, leaned my elbows on my knees, and stared down at her. "Did she offer any reason for that remarkable hypothesis?"

She kept reading and eventually said, "Well, if you can call it a reason, she says there doesn't seem to be any other explanation for why she would be at a place like this at that time on a Saturday night. She quotes some statistics: that a Hispanic girl murdered and raped in the Bronx in a lonely place of these characteristics is most likely to be a prostitute..."

She stopped reading and stared at me. She looked mad. I agreed. I felt mad too. "So basically she had no evidence and assumed because she was an Hispanic girl out late on a Saturday in the Bronx she was a whore."

"That's about the size of it."

I sighed and stood up. "This is not Hunts Point. It's one of the safest areas in the Bronx. Not just the Bronx, in New York. Whatever her statistics may say, the chances of finding a prostitute working this district are practically nonexistent."

"Plus, look at the way she was dressed. What was her line, Miss Demure? A flutter of the eyelashes is extra?"

I laughed. "Mmm... sounds appealing."

"Funny."

I joined her on the knoll. "Did they check NamUs?"

"There is no mention of that."

"Let's go talk to Detective Ibanez. I think this is a case of the same old same old, Dehan. A woman nobody cares about killed by a guy nobody cares about. You go through the motions, you don't get an immediate hit off the databases, so you file it under Don't Give a Damn and let it go cold." We started climbing back up the bank. I spoke over my shoulder as we climbed. "And let's look at women who were reported missing around that time. It will be tedious, but I reckon if we can get some idea of who she was, we'll get some idea why she died, and who killed her."

YOU COULD TELL Detective Veronica Ibanez liked to think of herself as badass. She didn't wait for us to find her, she came looking for us. She was small, all her movements were quick, and she chewed gum like she was in a hurry to get it chewed. She shouted to me as we walked into the detectives' room. "Yo! Stone! You want to talk to me?"

She said it as she walked across the room with her chin stuck in the air.

I smiled and frowned at the same time. "How'd you know?"

She arrived at our desks as I was pulling off my jacket. She had her hands in her jeans pockets and was chewing furiously. "Inspector told me you was looking at the Westchester whore . . ." She grinned and made a small noise that wanted to be a laugh but never made it. "I figured you'd wanna talk to me, get my view."

"Yeah. Grab a chair."

"I prefer to stand. I get restless sitting down. Whatcha wanna know?"

Dehan sighed, dropped into her chair, and opened her laptop.

I rested my ass against the desk. "What made you think she was a prostitute?"

She shrugged. "What else? She wasn't doin' voluntary work out there at that time of the night, was she?"

"That was it?"

"What else?" she said again. It was obviously her go-to analysis. "If it walks like a duck and it quacks like a duck, it's a duck!"

I shrugged and gave a small laugh. "But she didn't look like a duck. Her clothes were sober, demure even. She looked the picture of respectable middle class."

She made a "pfff!" sound. "You ever worked vice? I tell you, Stone, you should take a sabbatical and work vice for a year. It'll open your eyes. You get whores of every color, shape, size, and persuasion! Ask Mo . . ." Mo was laughing like an egg custard. "Hey, Mo, you're writing a thesis on the whole gamut of whoredom, ain't ya? You know 'em all, huh? You dirty bastard!" There was a moment of generalized hilarity. She turned back to me. "Believe me, pal. Clothes don't mean nothin'!"

I was about to ask her how, then, she knew what a duck looked like, but I could see the discussion turning circular, so I left it and moved on.

"I saw in the file you ran her prints and her DNA, but there's no mention of NamUs. Did you check on women reported missing . . . ?"

Before I could finish the question she gave a big shout of laughter. "Are you kidding me? Do you know how many files on missing women there are? One hundred thousand, my friend! *One hundred thousand!*" She did a weird thing with her neck, moving her head from side to side. "If you think I'm gonna bust my ovaries goin' through a hundred thousand files looking for a babe who is probably an illegal *anyway*, so she ain't gonna *be* in those files, you are plumb crazy. No way. You wanna do that, be my guest. I got more important things to do!"

I heard Dehan's voice from behind me. "More important than identifying a murdered girl?"

Before she could answer, I said, "What steps *did* you take to identify her, Veronica?"

"You know what we did. It's in the report. We ran her

through CODIS and IAFIS, and we spent a day canvassing the area. Nobody knew her, nobody had seen her."

I heard Dehan snort. "A whole day, huh? You sure earned your pay that week, Ibanez."

I glanced around at her and smiled. She was staring at her laptop. Ibanez looked at me. "You know what, Stone? I don't need this."

I nodded. "I know, you have important stuff to do."

"Take a hike. You got any questions, look in the report."

She went striding at speed back across the room, with her chin in the air. I turned back to Dehan. "What are you doing?"

"I'm checking the reports from the time to see if there is any mention of the position of the body."

"And?"

"So far I've read three reports. None of them says anything about the position of the victim." She sat back in her chair and linked her fingers behind her head. "Seems to me that, if the media had been told that it looked as though the body was going to be dumped into the water, they would have reported it." She shrugged. "You know, bodies floating down the river, that kind of stuff. Sort of thing the press like."

"I'm inclined to agree. But keep looking. I'm going to look for women reported missing May and June of 2016. Veronica is probably right. It probably runs into thousands. But first, let's go and report to *El Jefe*."

We climbed the stairs to the inspector's office, tapped, and were told to come in. He was standing at the window, spraying something onto his potted plants. He smiled benignly at us and gestured toward his chairs. "Sit, sit. I am just tending to my plants. All life is sacred, don't you think?"

Dehan said nothing so I spoke for both of us. "Can't argue with that, sir."

"No," he said, lowering himself into his chair with a sigh. "And if you did, you'd be wrong. So, how did you get on at Rikers? Has he got information of value? Or is he bluffing?"

Dehan answered. "It may be both, sir. He has something, but it may not be as valuable as he is trying to make out."

He frowned. "I see..."

I said, "He claims he was at the scene."

"In what capacity?"

"Well, that's just the thing, sir. He says he was enjoying a joint, lying on the grass looking at the stars, when he saw the killer arrive with the victim. He claims she was bound and gagged. He described the way her wrists were bound and, more important than that, he said that after the victim was killed, the killer tried to drag her to the river. That is a fact that, as far as we know, was never reported to the media."

He nodded. "Aha, so if he knows that, either he was there as a witness..."

"Or he did it."

"Indeed. So what are your next steps?"

I drew breath but Dehan spoke first. "We spoke to Detective Ibanez. She couldn't add anything to what was in the report. So we thought we would check how the murder was reported at the time and see if there is any reference to the body's being moved. If there isn't, then A, Wayne becomes our prime suspect, and B, the chances are good he has more information to give us. Also, we start trawling reports of missing women around May and June 2016."

He frowned. "That wasn't done in the original investigation?"

I shook my head once. "Nope."

He raised an eyebrow. "I see. May I suggest you also approach the PDs and sheriff's departments of New Jersey, Maryland, Pennsylvania, Connecticut, et cetera..."

I nodded. "All our immediate neighbors. Yes, we'll do that. How we proceed thereafter, sir, depends very much on what we find regarding how the media reported the case."

He leaned back in his chair. "That makes perfect sense, Detectives. Well done. I won't hold you up any longer. Good work."

As we left he was reaching for the internal phone. As I closed

FIRE FROM HEAVEN | 207

the door we heard him saying, "Ah, Detective Ibanez, could you come up and see me for a moment..."

We passed her on her way up. She and I made a point of ignoring each other, but Dehan said, "Going to see the Inspector, Ibanez? Say hi from me."

She didn't answer.

We worked through lunch; Dehan read every article she could find on the case and contacted the major TV news networks for any footage they had where the murder was reported. Meanwhile, I sent out a request to the neighboring PDs and sheriff's departments for missing persons reports on Hispanic females in their early to midtwenties, reported missing in late May or June 2016.

After that it was a matter of trawling, painstakingly, through the NamUs database. Ibanez had not exaggerated. There were approximately one hundred thousand cases of missing women over the age of twenty-one, and an extra two thousand three hundred people reported missing every day. My search criteria were pretty narrow, but even so there were thousands of files to work through.

By eight o'clock that evening I was beat. I rubbed my eyes, crunched my vertebrae, and looked at Dehan, who was leaning back with a pencil in her mouth, reading from the screen of her laptop.

I shrugged and shook my head. "I haven't found her. I need food and a bottle of wine."

She nodded for a while, still reading. Then she yawned and stretched, reached forward, and switched off the computer. "Me too." She rubbed her face with her hands and stared at me. "It was not reported, Stone. However Wayne Harris came by that information, it was not through the press." We stared at each other for a long moment, then she summed it up. "Either he has spoken to somebody who was there and told him what happened, or..." She shrugged and I nodded.

"He was there."

CHAPTER 3

By the time we got home it was almost nine o'clock. Dehan put a couple of pizzas in the oven while I pulled a cork from a bottle of wine, then fixed a couple of martinis, extra dry, while the wine breathed. As I placed her drink on the bar, Dehan said, "So, Sensei, how do you want to play it?"

I thought about it. "First drink, then dinner, then bed."

"Where's your red nose, Mr. Clown?"

I carried my drink to the sofa, kicked off my shoes, stretched out, and spoke to the ceiling. "I say we don't rush our fences. Wayne ain't going anywhere anytime soon." Dehan came over, nudged my feet aside with her ass, and sat on the arm of the sofa. I looked at her. "He's playing it like he has a strong hand. Maybe he has, but we can bluff. I don't want to give him a deal if I can avoid it."

She nodded. "So, before we go back to him we try to find out who she is. Then take it from there."

I nodded. "I think that makes sense."

There was a ping from my phone. She retrieved it from my jacket pocket and handed it to me.

I thumbed the screen. "Emails," I said. "Whadd'ya know. Philadelphia PD and Boston PD." I pulled myself into a sitting position and read: "Reported missing June first, 2016, Sonia Ibarri of Buttonwood Avenue, Maple Shade Township in Philly. Twenty-two at the time of her disappearance."

Her eyebrows rose up. "Sounds promising, if that's the right word."

"Hmmm . . . We'll find out tomorrow." I went to the next email. "Boston PD. Rosario Clemente, twenty-three at the time of her disappearance. Reported missing Sunday the twenty-second of May, 2016. One week after our victim was killed. Also a good candidate. Neither of them is called Angela."

Dehan shrugged. "It could have been her grandmother's cross. Could be a family heirloom. They both sound like they could be our girl."

"We'll go see them tomorrow, have a look at some pictures, and hope we don't have to show them any of Angela."

She nodded gravely, then gently punched my knee. "C'mon, big guy. Pizza's ready."

NEXT MORNING DEHAN phoned ahead to Alicia Clemente, Rosario's mother, and the Ibarris while I made breakfast, and by nine we were on the road to Boston. It was a three-hour drive, but we didn't talk much. We were in a somber mood. One hour in, Dehan, looking out at the woodlands and fields around New Haven, said, "It's hard to know what to hope for. You hope for a positive ID to be able to lay her soul to rest, and give some closure to the family. But you hope for a negative too, so you can give them some hope." She turned to look at me, with her aviators hiding her eyes. "We want truth and we want hope. It's a tough break when the truth robs you of hope."

There was no answer to that, so we drove on in silence.

At twelve we pulled into Dedham, in Norfolk County, on the southwest border of Boston. Their house was a large, attractive clapboard affair on Crowley Avenue, and backed onto a magnificent old Catholic church. I couldn't help wondering who on the town council had named the streets. Probably the same person who called the town "Dead Ham."

I followed Dehan up the stone steps to the porch and she rang on the bell. It was opened almost immediately by an attractive woman in her late forties or early fifties. She had made no effort to conceal the gray streaks in her black hair, which she had cut short. She was dressed in black Levi's and a denim shirt, and had a single string of pearls around her neck, which she fingered as she looked at us without speaking.

I said, "Mrs. Clemente?"

"Yes. Are you the detectives from New York?"

I nodded and showed her my badge. "I am Detective John Stone. This is my partner, Detective Carmen Dehan. May we come in?"

"Of course." She stepped back, holding the door. "Do you know something about Rosario?"

There was a hint of Latino in her accent, but it was more generic, cultured East Coast. Dehan said, "We don't know yet, Mrs. Clemente. That's what we hope you will help us find out."

She led us through a hall to a large, comfortable living room with dark wood floors, and two open sash windows set into a bow, overlooking Crowley Avenue. There were bookcases floor to ceiling in the alcoves on either side of an iron fireplace, and the occasional tables that flanked the old leather chairs and sofas all held large, interesting lamps—and more books: some open, all with bookmarkers in them. I noticed a couple were on architecture.

To the left of the door the room opened out to a set of French doors that gave onto a broad lawn. At the end of the lawn I could see the church. In front of the French doors there was a baby grand piano, and on it a photograph. I wondered if it was Rosario. Mrs. Clemente was gesturing us to sit, and saying, "Will you have some coffee?"

I shook my head as I sat on the sofa. "No, thank you. We

won't keep you long." She sat in the chair next to me, staring intently at my face. I said, "I realize you must have been through all this before, but it would be very helpful if you could tell us about Rosario, and the last time you saw her."

She sank back in the chair, her eyes abstracted. Outside the sun was bright and I could hear busy birdsong, but inside it was shaded and still.

She took a deep breath. "I raised Rosario alone. I was young when I had her. She was . . ." She made an expressive face. "A *mistake*! But she was the best mistake I ever made!" She laughed. "Bobby—that's her father—he was hot, you know?" She smiled at Dehan. "But I didn't want to *marry* him! Hell! I didn't want to have kids with him! We were at college, he was planning a career and so was I. But God decided he wanted me to have Rosario, so he busted the rubber and next thing I know I'm pregnant."

Her laughter was infectious. She flapped a hand at me. "You have to forgive me. I talk plain. I always have. It's got me into trouble sometimes, but hey! That's me. Anyway, Bobby panicked and ran, but my parents were fantastic and they helped me. Rosario grew up in a real close, loving family and . . ."

She paused, and suddenly her eyes were flooded with tears. She bit her lip and stared at me, with her head on one side, like she was begging me not to give her the news she feared I had brought.

Dehan said, "You had a good relationship with her."

She nodded, took another deep breath to steady herself. "Very good. People joked we were more like sisters than mother and daughter." She smiled and shook her head. "But it's not true. I was her mamma. And she is my little girl."

I leaned forward with my elbows on my knees. "Can you tell me about the last time you saw her?"

She gazed over at the open window with the fingers of her right hand resting on her pearls. "She had only recently graduated. She was clever, a real good student." She glanced at Dehan, like she felt they would share some kind of understanding about that. "She did architecture, like me. But she was interested in green, sustainable bio-architecture. It's a whole new field." She laughed again. "When I was a student we built things! Now they integrate materials!" She nodded, as though agreeing with some internal dialogue she had going on. "She was good, real good. So she got some interviews in New York..."

She shifted in her chair and frowned at me. "She applied only to small firms that were specializing in sustainable, eco-architecture. She didn't care about money. What she wanted to do was develop skills she could take to the Third World, because she believed a new model of sustainable economy would be born out there, like she said, from the roots up."

She took a big breath.

Dehan said, "She was an idealist."

Mrs. Clemente put a lopsided smile on her face and nodded. "She said she was a practical idealist. However, life teaches us there is no such thing. She was naïve." She shrugged. "But thank God for naïve people, right? Because they are the ones who do worthwhile things in this world. Pragmatists maintain the status quo. Dreams shake things up."

I gave a small laugh. "Maybe you have something there, Mrs. Clemente. She got some interviews in New York?"

"Yeah." She reached out and touched my foot. "I'm sorry. It's so nice to talk about her. All my friends are terrified of talking about her in case I cry. But it's a . . ." She shook her head and leaned forward toward Dehan. "It's a *fucking relief*!" She threw her head back and laughed. "Excuse me, but it is such a *fucking* relief to talk about her and laugh about her and *cry about her*! Why not? God gave us tears for a reason, right? So . . . !" She made an eloquent gesture with her hands, like things were flying around her head. "I am all over the place today, thinking about her. You asked . . . ?"

"Her interviews."

"Right. She had two. One was a smart outfit on Riverside Drive, on the Upper West Side in Manhattan. She wasn't so keen on that one. She thought the 'green' aspect with them was more

FIRE FROM HEAVEN | 213

for show. Then there was another one in Brooklyn that she was more hopeful about."

Dehan pulled a pen and notepad from her pocket. "Can you give us their addresses?" She wrote them down, then asked, "And were these both on the same day?"

"No, she wanted to spend a couple of days in New York. So she stayed with a friend."

Dehan stared at her a moment, waiting.

"Oh, um, Pam, Pam lived with her parents, Jason and Stella, give me a second and I'll remember. Hermany Avenue, twenty-two twenty, in the Bronx..."

I nodded and smiled. "I know it. It's not far from our precinct."

The words hung in the air like a bad omen. Outside the birds were still singing and the sun was still shining, but inside Mrs. Clemente had gone very still and very quiet, staring at me, taking in the significance of my words. Dehan was staring at me too.

I looked at her. "It runs into Zerega Avenue. Two hundred and twenty-two, would be about half a mile from the FedEx depot."

Mrs. Clemente asked in a dead voice, "What does that mean?"

I took a deep breath. "I'm not sure yet, Mrs. Clemente. Is that a photo of Rosario on the piano?"

She nodded. "Yes."

"May I have a look at it?"

She stood and walked quickly to the baby grand, picked up the picture in both hands, and brought it back, clasped to her bosom. Dehan got up and sat next to me on the sofa. Mrs. Clemente sat on the other side and handed me the picture. We all three stared at it together. The girl in it was beautiful. It was a graduation photo. She had her cap and gown on, and she was smiling into the camera. Her hair was black and her eyes were large, dark and humorous, like her mother's. She was full of life and enthusiasm, and dreams and hopes, but she wasn't Angel.

"This is not the girl we've found, Mrs. Clemente."

"Not . . . ? But the girl you found, is she alive . . . ?"

I shook my head. "No. The girl we found was murdered, two years ago."

"At the same time that Rosario was in New York?"

"About half a mile away from where she was staying."

"Oh, *Dios Santo* . . . !"

Dehan reached over and took her hand. "Mrs. Clemente, why was Rosario reported missing here instead of New York?"

"Because she left Pamela's house on Saturday morning, on her way home. Pamela left her at the bus station. She saw her get on the bus. Rosario was a very impulsive, spontaneous, independent girl. That's the way I brought her up. It's the way my parents brought me up too. I always thought maybe she got off somewhere on the way, to look at the sea or whatever. But she would have called, and by Saturday night I was worried. I called the cops, and by the time I filed the report it was, I guess, one o'clock on Sunday morning."

"So the report was filed here."

She nodded. "You think there may be a connection?"

I sighed. "It's impossible to say at this stage, Mrs. Clemente. Over fifty percent of the population of the Bronx is Hispanic, about half of them are women . . ." I shrugged. "What look to us like parallels may just be statistical facts. Let's not jump to conclusions just yet. We will look into this, we'll talk to Pamela, and if you'll give us permission to check her bank and phone records we'll try and build a picture of what happened on Friday and Saturday."

She nodded. "Of course." She fought to control the tears, frowning as though trying to make sense out of what was inherently absurd and cruel. "She is dead, isn't she?"

I held her eye and felt momentarily exhausted. "I wish I could answer that for you, Mrs. Clemente. I honestly don't know."

"The not knowing is almost worse . . . May God forgive me."

I nodded. "I know. We'll be in touch as soon as we have any

news. Is there somebody you can call on? Today is going to be tough. You'll be remembering..."

She echoed my nod. "You're kind. I have my work. Tonight I'll go and dine with my parents. We'll get through it together."

I smiled and patted her hand. "Sure. Feel free to call us anytime."

Dehan took a photograph of the picture with her phone and we stood. I hesitated a moment, then asked, "There is one thing, Mrs. Clemente. Have you anything—a lock of hair..."

She closed her eyes. "DNA..."

"Yes. Just..." I trailed off.

She turned and went to a dresser. There she opened a drawer and took out a small tin. She brought it over and handed it to me. "It's her first milk tooth. When you're done with it..."

"We'll bring it back to you."

Dehan gave her two kisses on the cheek and they hugged like they were family or old friends, then she showed us to the door and we made our way to the Jag, sitting old, sober, and burgundy in the May sunshine. I climbed in behind the wheel and watched Mrs. Clemente close the door. Dehan climbed in beside me.

"Is there any worthwhile profession," I asked the world at large, and Dehan in particular, "that does not involve dealing with human tragedy?"

"Lots, geology, physics, architecture... Stone?"

I turned to face her. "Yeah..."

"How much of your life have you not told me about?"

I grimaced and nodded a lot. "Why?"

"The way you talked to her. She said that the not knowing was worse than knowing..." She frowned and shook her head. "You said you knew. Sure, we're cops. All cops know that's true. But the way you said it, you *do* know. You know that from experience."

I shrugged. "One day, Dehan, but not today."

I turned the key and the big old engine growled. I spun the

wheel and we turned back, south, toward Philadelphia and the Ibarri family.

After about half an hour she reached over and squeezed my knee. It was a gesture that made me smile. I looked at her. She was smiling back at me, with the wind whipping her hair across her beautiful face. "You don't have to," she said. "You're an old, Anglo-Saxon dinosaur. I get that, and I like it. But when you're ready, I'm here."

I nodded. "I know."

And we drove on in comfortable silence.

Scan the QR code below to purchase TO KILL UPON A KISS.
Or go to: righthouse.com/to-kill-upon-a-kiss

Made in the USA
Middletown, DE
11 January 2025

69311833R00135